Small tinges of red appeared on her cheeks

"There's nothing to be ashamed of in enjoying a kiss, Princess," Adam warned quite seriously.

"I didn't!" Serena denied hotly.

"That's not what that sensuous mouth of yours was telling me," he reminded her ruthlessly, his gaze moving to her lips. "Perhaps we should put it to the test again."

"What do you want from me?" she demanded, the arrogant tilt of her head a provocation in itself.

"I'm surprised you haven't worked that out yet," he replied cryptically. "But no matter, Princess, the light will dawn one day."

"You're mad," Serena gasped. She felt she would hit him. And catching the sardonic gleam in his eyes as they traveled over the rapid rise and fall of her breasts, she almost did.

WELCOME
TO THE WONDERFUL WORLD
OF *Harlequin Presents*

Interesting, informative and entertaining,
each Harlequin Presents portrays an appealing
and original love story. With a varied array
of settings, we may lure you on an African safari,
to a quaint Welsh village, or an exotic Riviera
location—anywhere and everywhere that adventurous
men and women fall in love.

As publishers of Harlequin Presents, we're
extremely proud of our books. Since 1949,
Harlequin Enterprises has built its publishing
reputation on the solid base of quality and
originality. Our stories are the most popular
paperback romances sold in North America; every
month, eight new titles are released and sold at
nearly every book-selling store in Canada and the
United States.

A free catalog listing all Harlequin Presents
can be yours by writing to the

HARLEQUIN READER SERVICE,
(In the U.S.) P.O. Box 52040, Phoenix, AZ 85072-2040
(In Canada) Stratford, Ontario, N5A 6W2

We sincerely hope you enjoy reading
this Harlequin Presents.

Yours truly,

THE PUBLISHERS
Harlequin Presents

ALISON FRASER

princess

Harlequin Books

TORONTO • NEW YORK • LONDON
AMSTERDAM • PARIS • SYDNEY • HAMBURG
STOCKHOLM • ATHENS • TOKYO • MILAN

Harlequin Presents first edition June 1984
ISBN 0-373-10697-1

Original hardcover edition published in 1984
by Mills & Boon Limited

CHAPTER ONE

THE sun should be brighter, she thought. And it shouldn't rain so much, should it? It was never this cold when her father was there—or this quiet, either. Maybe he would come back soon, maybe they would walk through their favourite vineyard and work up an appetite for sharing a king-sized pizza. Maybe . . .

But why was it so hard to remember? Why was it so cold?

Bleak, was Adam's verdict. Real Brontë country, down to the wind threatening storm that had carried away the bare eulogy at the graveside earlier that afternoon. Climbing out of the passenger seat of an elderly Rover, he turned up his collar against it and let his eyes range dispassionately over his late aunt's home, Simmonds Hall.

Mr Alexander, the solicitor, came to stand at his side and observe. 'Quite an impressive house, Mr Carmichael.'

'Really.' It was a noncommittal sound. The house was large, certainly, over a dozen narrow casement windows running the length of the upper storey, but the local stone was badly weathered, its ivy covering grown rampant rather than picturesque.

Adam hoped he had misconstrued his required presence at the will reading. The house's windswept isolation held no appeal and its size and neglected state stamped it a white, or perhaps more appropriately, grey elephant. With a touch of irreverence he prayed that his widowed, childless aunt had been fond of cats or juvenile delinquents or some other worthy cause that might have worked in his disfavour.

More familiar with their surroundings, the old solicitor led the way through the darkened hallway to the library, bare of furniture save for a long oak table flanked by several high-backed chairs. The air in the room was stale and oppressive, the heavy curtains closed to mark a death in the family.

'Do you mind?' Adam asked perfunctorily, then presumed on his position as one half of the dead woman's surviving family to draw back the curtains. The cold grey daylight made the room stark but tolerable. He turned back to Mr Alexander. 'Will this take long?'

The older man looked up from the papers he was sorting with a faintly surprised expression. Curbing some of the impatience in his tone, Adam went on to explain, 'I had hoped to be back in London by early evening.'

At this the solicitor's surprise hardened to shock—presumably for his unseemly hurry to dispense with the rituals of death, Adam mused.

'Why, Mr Carmichael . . . I had assumed that you would be staying . . . at least overnight,' Mr Alexander muttered agitatedly. 'Although I did not draw up her last will, my late client expressed a wish that you, her nephew, should take care of her . . . um . . . affairs.'

It was a repetition of what his mother had said when pressing Adam into representing her at the funeral. At the time he had considered it merely an excuse for her delegation of the duty.

'Do you really think it necessary?' Adam pursued with heavy reluctance to stay even one night in Yorkshire.

Mr Alexander's eyes almost boggled behind his round gold-rimmed spectacles. In his worst imaginings of Adam Carmichael, based on a jaundiced view of bestselling writers, he had not anticipated this.

'Of course, Mr Carmichael, it's your decision entirely. In the circumstances, however, to settle so delicate a matter by postal communication alone, would be—well . . .' the solicitor, visibly flurried, trailed off.

Unable to see anything particularly delicate about winding up his aunt's estate, nevertheless Adam gave in with a measure of good grace. He had no desire to enter a lengthy legal correspondence.

'I understand. Is there a telephone I could use?' he asked. 'I must cancel a social engagement.'

'Certainly,' the solicitor breathed on a note of relief, and indicating a door in the far corner of the room, added, 'You will find the adjoining room quite private.'

It was a sitting room, the furniture cumbersome and lacking in style, the décor chillingly drab. From what Adam had seen so far, his aunt, or perhaps her first husband—that last Simmonds of Simmonds Hall—had had very austere taste.

He sat for a moment, thinking about the dead woman. He had met Andrea Templeton once briefly, and recalled a tall, striking woman with titian hair and a brittle laugh. He had neither liked nor disliked her; indeed he knew precious little about her, for his mother had been more vague than usual on the subject of her half-sister. Concluding that he had been chosen to take care of her affairs by default as her only male relative, he gave up his concentration to the telephone.

Even at this relatively late hour, Julia sounded sleepy and languid when she answered, but immediately dropped all casualness when he identified himself. He cut into her enthusiastic outpourings to explain why he was ringing, listened impassively to her petulant protests at being stood up, as she termed it, and then hung up on her when her tone became strident.

Julia Montague, the latest in a long line of girl-friends, was a very attractive woman in the physical sense, but Adam had no intention of dancing to her, or any woman's, shrill tune. At the beginning of their relationship he had made it plain that he was not in the marriage stakes, and it was now reaching the stage where his interest was rapidly cooling. He made a mental note to get some 'it was nice knowing you' jewellery that would satisfy her acquisitive nature, and then completely dismissed her from his mind.

When Adam returned to the library, the lawyer was no longer alone. Seated on the far side of the reading table was a schoolgirl, dressed in plain grey jersey and white blouse, her head bent forward, a rash of fair hair obscuring her face.

And as Mr Alexander rose from his chair and turned to Adam, he gained perfect but belated understanding of the other's mystified expression. What he had taken for callousness had, quite remarkably in his eyes, been total ignorance.

'Mr Carmichael, this is Mrs Templeton's stepdaughter, Serena,' he hastily performed the necessary introduction and then in a markedly slower tone, addressed the girl, 'Mr Carmichael is your mother's nephew, Serena.'

'I'm glad to meet you, Serena,' Adam responded with a neutral politeness, despite being more than a little put out by this large detail omitted by his mother in her sketchy account of her sister's life.

Head still bowed, the girl ignored both his outstretched hand and his greeting. Adam was first stunned and then angry at the blatant rudeness, but catching the plea in the solicitor's eyes, he bit back any retort. His attention was distracted by the entry of a large cheerful woman bearing a tray of tea and finely-cut sandwiches. This time he was acknowledged with a broad pleasant smile.

'Will that be all, sir?' the newcomer enquired as she placed a cup of tea and sandwich in front of the young girl, directing another quick curious glance in Adam's direction.

'Perhaps you could see that everything is ready for Mr Carmichael. He will be staying overnight, Mrs Baker,' the solicitor courteously dismissed her as he became increasingly conscious of Adam's fixed stare on the top of a golden head that remained rigidly still and unresponsive, despite the reassuring squeeze her lifeless hand had received from the departing housekeeper.

Shuffling papers about, he waited until the door was firmly shut before clearing his throat and proceeding tonelessly, 'I, Andrea Felicia Templeton, being of sound mind, do make this my last will and testament. To my beloved stepdaughter, Serena Jane Templeton, I leave my jade ring and necklace which, in her own simple way, she admired so much . . . The residue of my estate I leave to my nephew, Adam Carmichael, under the condition that he accepts legal responsibility for my stepdaughter, and in the belief that he is the most suitable person so to do.'

Alexander paused, throwing a glance between the other occupants of the room; the girl's face was still hidden by the straggle of her hair, and he gained no assurance from the cool implacability of Adam's. Signs of shock or displeasure would somehow have been more comforting.

His reluctance became even more heavily pronounced as he read on, 'As a result of injuries sustained in a motor accident, my stepdaughter is . . . mentally retarded and I therefore have no objection to her being placed in an appropriate private institution.' By the end Mr Alexander's embarrassment was almost palpable. He murmured apologetically, 'Most distressing, I'm afraid.'

The eyes of both men now rested expectantly on the girl, but she gave no indication that she had understood or even heard the blunt phrasing that applied to her. Eventually, sighing, the older man rose stiffly and summoned the housekeeper with the old-fashioned bellpull beside the fireplace.

'Will you escort Serena to her room, please, Mrs Baker,' he instructed gravely. 'I think she's tired.'

Gently touching the girl's shoulder, the woman encouraged, 'Come along, my lamb,' and without lifting her head, the girl automatically shuffled out of the room.

Adam observed her retreating figure, formless in her ill-fitting clothes, with clinical interest, and when the door closed behind them, said with soft sardonicism, 'The delicate matter?'

'I must apologise, I didn't realise that . . .'

'Scarcely your fault,' Adam reassured succinctly while mentally squaring the blame on his mother's shoulders. 'As you have probably gathered, my knowledge of my aunt is extremely limited. Presumably she is the child of the second husband?'

'Yes, he died in the accident to which my late client referred. Tragic loss of a fine artist,' Mr Alexander murmured dolefully, and at Adam's frown of incomprehension, enlarged, 'Graham Templeton—perhaps you have heard of him?'

'*Graham* Templeton?' repeated Adam with mild incredulity, for he had one of the man's paintings in the study of his service flat—a portrait he had bought several years ago from a small London gallery. Seeing it in the window, he had been struck by the serenity of the woman's face, a beauty that was not flamboyant but somehow compelling. In reply to the solicitor's oblique glance, he remarked, 'I have one of his paintings. A much undervalued man.'

'Indeed yes. He preferred obscurity to recognition and did little to promote his work.' The tone revealed more than a passing admiration. 'I regret my acquaintanceship with Mr Templeton was so short.'

'When was the accident?' Adam quizzed.

'Let me see, it happened about two years after the marriage,' he matched Adam's matter-of-fact tone, since the young man was certainly no grieving relative, 'and that would have been slightly over seven years ago.'

'So the girl has been in that condition for five years,' Adam calculated.

'Not exactly,' Mr Alexander said hesitantly. 'The girl was undoubtedly ill when her stepmother took her home from the hospital, but . . .'

'But?' Adam pressed.

'Before the accident Serena was a bright, gifted child.'

The solicitor strove to overcome a dislike for speculation and partially succeeded, continuing, 'In the first half year after the accident, *I* did not perceive any signs of mental impairment in the girl, although she was, of course, deeply affected by her loss. They were very close, even for a father and daughter.'

Adam was not sure what he was meant to make, if anything, of this sombre speech.

'What are you implying, Mr Alexander?'

The old solicitor removed his glasses and began to wipe them. It was a distracted action, as he wavered on the verge of saying more before reverting to his usual cautious stance.

'I did not wish to imply anything,' he replied flatly, replacing his spectacles. 'I was merely stating an impression.'

Adam respected his reticence and asked a more pertinent question. 'What is the medical opinion on her condition?'

'The local doctor suggested that the girl might be suffering the delayed effects of a severe blow she received on the skull,' the other relayed.

'And the specialist?'

'Specialist?' Alexander echoed.

'Brain specialist,' Adam expanded abruptly, and when it was met with a telling silence, he said in disbelief, 'She hasn't been examined by one?'

A shade defensively, as though he was guilty of the omission himself, the solicitor admitted, 'Your aunt was adverse to consulting one. She appeared to believe that Serena would get better in time . . . of her own accord.'

'So the girl has had no treatment?'

'The doctor did prescribe some sleeping tablets for the girl's recurring nightmares about the accident, and for when she became excitable during the day,' Mr Alexander informed him, almost gratified by how hard the younger man was pushing him on the matter. He had, however, mistaken Adam Carmichael's practical streak for compassion.

But Adam's disgust was real enough as he disapproved, 'Sedatives for a child?'

'For her own safety, I believe,' Alexander replied. 'I understand she began to wander in the night, and although Mrs Templeton gave strict instructions to lock every door and window, she managed to get out one night and the police found her at dawn, lost and feverish, on the hills about four miles away.'

'Running away?' Adam sharply spoke his thoughts aloud and was himself surprised by the direction they had taken. For a moment Mr Alexander's narrative had conjured up an image of his aunt as gaoler instead of protector.

'From what?'

Adam shrugged, 'From Andrea, I suppose.'

Mr Alexander looked troubled for a second by what was obviously a new idea, but his reply had a definite ring. 'If I may say so, Mr Carmichael, that is extremely unlikely. Your aunt was devoted to the girl's interests. According to the housekeeper, she literally waited on her hand and foot.'

'A trifle over-protective, then?' Adam suggested.

'Perhaps,' Mr Alexander allowed. 'Serena had reputedly deteriorated since Mrs Templeton's last illness.'

'Does she still take medication?' He met the solicitor's eyes as he shook his grey head, and he was positive that the old man was thinking the same as he—the girl no longer needed any artificial depressants.

Indeed there was more than a touch of hopelessness in Mr Alexander's tentative, 'I wonder if you would care to venture an opinion on the girl's mental state—as a relative outsider?'

After minimal consideration Adam replied, 'Judging from the child's total lack of reaction to that rather bluntly worded will, I would say she appears autistic—in as far as my layman's opinion counts for anything.' The slight, almost imperceptible upward movement of her head at the mention of the jade jewellery came to mind, only to be dismissed as insignificant. 'Does your opinion differ?'

Mr Alexander removed his glasses once more and rubbed his eyes in a gesture of weariness, before affirming, 'Based on her behaviour today, I am forced to agree with you.'

'What is the girl's mental age?' Adam enquired, mind already running ahead to practicalities.

'I really couldn't say,' the solicitor sighed, and with a return to formality, 'Have you made any preliminary decision on how you would like to proceed? I must advise you that your legacy is dependent on your becoming, at the very least, Serena's guardian.'

Adam forbore from mentioning that he had no need of his aunt's worldly goods to supplement his considerable private income.

'I imagine she can be found a place in a school for backward children.' It sounded cool and detached.

'I'm afraid it isn't quite that simple, Mr Carmichael.' Alexander moved from legal dryness to abrupt coldness. 'Serena is now too old for that sort of establishment. She will very shortly be nineteen.'

'Good God, I thought her fourteen at most—from the little I saw of her,' Adam muttered disbelievingly. 'If she's that old, why is she dressed like that? Surely her mother could afford clothes that fitted better, to say nothing of the style!'

His gaze encompassed the antique cases, containing richly bound books, and the sparse but expensive furniture to stress his point.

'Her *step*mother wished to underline her youth and make her as plain as possible. To avoid any chance of her arousing ... er ... romantic interest,' Mr Alexander explained, his tone reflecting some doubt, 'although I believe Serena has not been outside the grounds for some years.'

It seemed ridiculous to Adam that the withdrawn hunched figure should be considered as potentially attractive. With a shrewdness that jolted the other man he commented, 'You didn't like my aunt very much, did you, Mr Alexander?'

The elderly solicitor seemed to waver between a frank response and one he deemed professionally correct. The latter won out as he said stiffly, 'My connection with Mrs Templeton was of a strictly business nature.'

His attitude was what Adam had expected, but he was confident that he had read the solicitor accurately.

'What do you suggest I do about the girl?'

'Perhaps you could stay a few days and get to know Serena?' Mr Alexander proposed.

Again Adam picked up the old man's thoughts; clearly Mr Alexander wanted him to make more than a legal commitment to the girl but would doubt he was the sort of man to take an interest in one of life's waifs and strays. And Adam had no grounds on which to protest, since his life, dedicated to the pursuit of pleasure and only occasionally interrupted by a few months of concentrated work on a novel, had no room for lost causes.

'Perhaps.' The terse response gave no promises.

'Well, I'd better be going,' Mr Alexander was beginning to view the possibility of Adam taking a personal interest in the girl as a lost cause also. Shoving documents into his briefcase with less than his usual meticulousness, he added, 'I would be grateful if you could dispose of your aunt's private papers, as you think fit.'

'Of course,' Adam nodded.

Escorting Mr Alexander to his car, as much to get some fresh air as out of courtesy, he delayed in the forecourt in spite of the steady rain. Without conscious intention, he raised his eyes to the upper storey.

A small blonde head was pressed against one of the

windows, features blurred by the water streaming down the pane. She seemed to be staring down at him, and he returned her interest for a full minute. He tried a smile; the distorted face neither moved nor changed, disturbing in its immobility.

He discovered the lounge opposite the library, and poured himself a large whisky, pulling loose his black tie. Sitting in an armchair close to the lit fire, he stretched his long legs and stared broodingly into the flames, alternately wishing himself three hundred miles from the mausoleum of a house and condemning his mother for embroiling him in this situation. Even allowing for her aversion to any form of unpleasantness, she might at least have outlined the circumstances for him before he had been burdened with the responsibility for that lifeless child—who undoubtedly was oblivious to the problem she presented. Oblivious to about everything, he finally judged.

In fact Adam's keen perception had, for once, let him down: for the girl in question, while sitting with perfect stillness before that upstairs window on which her stare was frozen, was transmitting a message. To the woman who meant to keep a hold on her, even in death.

'I've seen him now,' she said silently, 'standing tall and erect in the courtyard. *Your* dark emissary who stands there in the rain staring up at his property—at me. But *I* know what he is . . .' and she smiled in her bitterness.

Adam rose at seven, irritable and unrefreshed. A fastidious dresser, he disliked having to re-wear the same shirt and was relieved to find a collection of worn but clean shirts in the base of the walnut wardrobe. The cotton stripe was hardly his usual style and was tight across his broad shoulders.

The clothes and toiletries in the adjoining bathroom had to be Templeton's, and Adam was critical of the sentimental preservation of the personal effects of the deal. Within days of his own father's fatal heart attack, his mother had neatly packed his numerous business suits, shirts and ties, and sent them to the nearest Oxfam shop. He had walked in on her doing so and stayed just long enough to see her tears staining a silk dinner shirt that was being folded and unfolded in her abstracted grief.

Profoundly moved, perhaps for the last time in his life, he had wanted to comfort, but in his own confusion and overwhelming sense of loss, the right words had not come, and his father's family, large and close-knit, had rallied round and provided the support his mother had needed at the time.

Adam, at barely twenty, found himself to be a very rich young man; public school training and the reserved, self-contained nature of an only child had inhibited any outward display of his very real grief for a father he had regarded as infallible, and he had been too young to see the event in anything but an intensely personal way.

He had never returned to the economics course he had been following at Cambridge, and for a time it had seemed to the Carmichael family, initially shocked and then frankly disapproving, that the young man they had seen as quiet and studious was intent on going through the money his highly industrious father had amassed, as fast as he possibly could.

Adam brushed down the crisp black hair that just touched the collar of the borrowed shirt and smiled mockingly at his good-looking reflection in the bathroom mirror. It had been a crazy time, changing fast cars and women the moment the latest model had lost its sheen of newness, and recklessly courting danger in the company of other young socialites of the 'sixties with more money than sense.

In retrospect, he realised he had been overreacting to his father's premature death, but he didn't consider that episode of his life entirely wasted. From the experiences, he had written his first book, partially tongue in cheek, and it had been hailed as an accurate representation of the mores of a lost spoilt generation.

The critical acclaim had pleased rather than excited Adam, but it had gone a long way to redeeming him in his mother's eyes, for she saw the writing as a sign of his preparing to settle down. That had been wishful thinking. For although Adam had matured out of his taste for bedding every attractive girl who came his way and the feverish lifestyle, he had become cynical in the process, and much of that hard core of cynicism was directed at himself. Charming when he chose to be, he could also be one of the most selfish bastards he knew.

And with that damning self-analysis, he descended the stairs to the study and telephoned Leeds for the times of the infrequent trains that stopped at Rippondale, the nearest village. There was one at noon he could easily make.

After a leisurely breakfast, however, he was not so lucky in contacting Mr Alexander. Disgruntled to find the solicitor was attending another funeral, Adam wondered how many clients the old man had left, considering the rate at which he seemed to be reading wills. Nevertheless he was reluctant to communicate his decision second-hand and arranged with the clerk that the solicitor should come to the house as soon as possible.

Several phone calls later, he finally located a car hire firm in Leeds willing to deliver a car to the Hall so that he was no longer at the mercy of public transport.

And then he was left, with time and silence and his thoughts, and insidiously they returned to an image of his young step-cousin, slumped and inert in the library chair. The housekeeper had pushed her cup of tea almost to the edge of the table, but if the movement had been in Serena's line of vision, it had made no impression on the girl. Throughout the reading of the will, the tea had remained untouched.

Her stepmother had described her condition as retardation. To Adam that term suggested slowness rather than the apparent . . . nothingness he had witnessed yesterday—as though the spirit had flown and left behind an empty shell. The uncharacteristically lyrical thought lingered to disturb before Adam became irritated with himself for playing amateur psychiatrist.

Damn Alexander for not being available, he cursed as he strode out into the hallway and shrugging into his suit jacket, slammed out of the house and into what he assumed must be normal Yorkshire weather, blustery even at the approach of summer.

He was unconscious of jade green eyes that followed his progress across the front yard to the outbuildings some two hundred yards from the house—eyes that saw but did not recognise, for Serena Jane Templeton had already pushed yesterday to the back of her mind, and now used the tall, striding figure to initiate one of her daydreams.

Her father was going to the stables. Perhaps he would take her riding today. They both liked it when the wind was high, fresh on their faces and streaming through their hair. He'd give her a head start because her horse was smaller, and they'd race to the top of the hill and stay there for hours, like a couple of truants talking over past adventures.

And he would hold her close and promise that better times were coming . . . soon, very soon.

The stables were divided into four stalls, unoccupied now of course, but Adam noticed that the tackle was spotlessly clean. As he fingered the quality leather of a saddle, it brought back pleasant memories of long summer days riding over the Downs with his cousins.

'No horses now, you know,' a gruff male voice stated the obvious.

Adam wheeled round to observe the man who had silently crept up on him. 'You're . . . ?'

'Brocklehurst, the gardener.' The reply was brusque.

Adam guessed him to be an age past retirement, as he took in an untidy thatch of white hair above a weatherbeaten, deeply-lined face.

'I'm . . .'

'I know who you be, Mr Carmichael.' For his age the man was exceptionally fit: in one easy movement he removed the saddle from Adam's reach and placed it in the tack room. The action could have been construed as rude.

'Someone keeps all this stuff in good condition,' Adam declared with a measure of curiosity, indicating the tackle.

'I do. Was groom once for the Hall. Never know when t'll be needed again,' Brocklehurst responded, and this time there was no mistaking the man's truculence. 'Never know when t'young miss will want to come out riding again.'

Adam estimated that five years must have passed since the young miss had been on a horse, making the old man's assertion totally ridiculous. Was the whole household bewitched by the girl? Last night after dinner the housekeeper had come to the lounge to plead on Serena's behalf, and Adam had listened with barely concealed impatience while the kindly matron made the girl sound like the sleeping princess of fairytales. And now Brocklehurst's hostility told him he had been ringed as the heartless villain who presented some sort of threat to her.

Were they all deaf, dumb and blind to the girl's state? Well, he wasn't. The girl needed professional care and attention which she couldn't get surrounded by old family retainers who pretended everything was normal.

Exasperated, he swung on his heel and left the old Yorkshireman, who was now painstakingly bringing a shine to a metal stirrup. He circled the house, and branched off as he caught sight of another outbuilding set lower than the house where the grass slope at the back gave way to woodland. It was square and more modern than the other buildings—and its largely glass roof marked it as Graham Templeton's studio specially built for the short time he had lived here.

He tried both doors. Unbelievably the side door was open—unbelievably, because there was a stack of canvasses leaning against the far wall. Didn't these people realise the potential value of the paintings left so casually?

Slowly he perused the paintings. They were good—very good. Added to the four examples of the man's work he had already seen, they confirmed his opinion that Graham Templeton had been a man of considerable talent.

The portrait of his second wife, concealed at the back, was especially arresting, for it caught the general impression of a proud, striking woman who was very much in control of her life, but the mouth subtly hinted at something else. With a few strokes of red, the artist had captured a latent weakness—or was it cruelty? Both, Adam decided. Impossible to tell if it represented a distorted view of the artist's or an accurate portrayal of his aunt, he surmised. Whichever, he felt no stirring to add it to his collection—its effect was powerful and unsettling.

When he returned to the house, he sought out Mrs Baker.

'I'd like to see Serena,' he ordered coolly, betraying none of the impulsiveness that had prompted the idea.

Mrs Baker's head shot up and her hands stilled in their task. Her jaw literally dropped. 'But, sir . . .'

'Yes, Mrs Baker?' Adam lifted an enquiring brow.

'W-well, sir,' the housekeeper stammered in her surprise, rubbing nervous hands up and down the front of her large flowered apron, 'I can take you up to her room, but I don't think she'll speak to you. Nothing personal, you understand. She's just very . . . shy,' she finished lamely.

Adam's rigid unwavering stare told Alice Baker the

choice was not hers to make. Her late mistress had had the same dark eyes that would fix on one, and communicate impatience, disapproval or dislike without having to say a word. Hurriedly she washed her hands and hung up her apron on the pantry door, briskly instructing Lizzie, the maid, standing with mouth gaping, to get on with the lunch.

Wordlessly Adam followed her plump figure upstairs, and Mrs Baker would have been even more surprised if she had known their thoughts ran parallel as they trod the corridor to the girl's bedroom. What did he, an unsympathetic stranger, hope to achieve?

Mrs Baker knocked on the door, but any hopes of monitoring the meeting were dashed as Adam inclined his head in a gesture of polite dismissal.

The room was dark and gloomy, rain now beating a regular tattoo on the windows. At first he thought it empty, as it was filled with an unnatural silence, but then he saw the girl sitting at the far end, motionless and staring out over the yard. He coughed lightly to announce his presence, but her back gave no sign of recognising it.

His eyes shifted round the room, austere and cheerless as the rest of the house, bare of possessions or ornaments except for two gilt-edged photograph frames on a chest of drawers.

The man he identified as Graham Templeton, a colour supplement having run an article about his work some years earlier. A quiet, unassuming man, his hair greyed by the time the photograph had been taken and a suggestion of humour about the mouth and eyes.

The face of the woman, however, was a relevation, for it was the model for the painting he himself owned, the one titled simply 'Serenity'; it had not occurred to him that he possessed the portrait of the man's first wife.

With the frame still in his hands, he approached the slight figure, yet even when he was within a foot of her chair she did not seem to be aware of him. He felt invisible, an unpleasant sensation.

He searched for an opening and asked with a deliberate slowness, 'Is this a picture of your mother?'

Apparently he had spoken the magic word, for the girl wheeled round and violently snatched the picture from his grasp. The wild look in the large vivid green eyes shook him, but he was more startled when he took in her full face. In feature it was a replica of his 'Serenity', with the same breathtaking bone-structure. The very fact that her face was so familiar made her savage expression and bone-thinness all the more remarkable. It was not a natural slimness, he appraised, but nearly a state of emaciation. Her hair, long and very fair, was tangled wildly, and looked as though it was never combed. But despite the fierceness, Adam was momentarily transfixed by a sense of beauty.

The transition from vibrant awareness to total blank-ness was almost instantaneous, like a light had shone too brightly and then snapped out. She shielded her precious photograph, arms locked tightly around it. The reasoning eluded him, but he knew she had expected him to take it forcibly from her; the fingers curling round her upper arms must have been inflicting pain, for long uncut nails were digging into her flesh.

Adam looked long and hard at the top of her head, and felt a wave of pity wash over him, so strong he had to swallow the constriction in his throat. In slow motion, as though he was dealing with a frightened cornered animal, he drew up a twin to her hard wooden chair and placed it next to hers.

'Please look at me.' Nothing. He extended his hand and she did not resist the light pressure of his index finger tilting her head upwards, but the blankness persisted.

'My name's Adam. I'm your mother's . . . stepmother's nephew.' As an attempt at reassurance it failed miserably, for it had her gripping the frame even closer to her chest.

'I'm not going to take your mother's picture away. She was very beautiful.'

Adam detected the merest flicker of an eyelid.

'I want to help you,' he vowed quietly, and was surprised at how true his simple statement was, no matter what cold rationality had decided earlier. He sifted through what the housekeeper had said about the girl. Hadn't there been something about her only interest being in sketching? 'If you come downstairs with me and have lunch, we can talk about your future. Perhaps you'd like to show me your drawing. I like looking at drawings.'

Her shocking reply was a whisper but clear and precise for all that. 'Don't patronise me!'

Green eyes were suddenly alive with defiance as he registered her words with cold alarm. It was exactly what he had been doing, talking to her as though she was mentally deficient, and her cool incisive tone belied this. He began to feel very much out of his depth.

'I'm sorry. I meant to be . . .'

'Kind to the poor retarded girl. Don't bother. Just leave me alone,' she clipped out each word, mimicking his slow deliberate speech. 'I know about you, understand?'

He didn't, but he had the oddest impression that she had really meant 'I know you' rather than 'I know about you'. Either way, it didn't make much sense.

'Did my aunt mention me? You must miss her a lot now . . .'

Laughter, cutting and humourless, stopped him dead. It was a far from pleasant sound—a sacrilege coming from so angelic a face.

'Oh, I miss her . . . just as she knew I would. That's why my *beloved* stepmother left you to me in her will.'

Again she pronounced this with a definite lucidity, but still it made no sense.

'I'm not with you, Serena.'

His tone, uneven and rattled, urged her for an explanation, but she confined herself to, 'No, you're not.' Then she laughed a second time, only the laughter cracked and splintered, and for a second it seemed it would turn to tears, but she shut her eyes very tightly and when they flickered open once more, the blankness had returned.

Adam desperately wanted her to explain her apparently meaningless statements, but she was gone from him, her face turned back to the window, indifferent to his presence. It was a trick, but real all the same. He wanted to shake her so that she would return to him, complete the absurd conversation she had left hanging in mid-air, but wherever her mind was, it was not in this room with him. And scarcely conscious of it, he felt some of the compassion for her change to a fine formless resentment that began to govern his attitude towards her.

Unable to see a way over the impenetrable wall the girl built round her at will, he left in silence, but with a head full of pointed, pointless riddles. He retrieved his copy of the will from the study desk, and for a long time pondered over the phrase—'the most suitable person so to do'—and was left still asking the question 'Why me?'

By no stretch of the imagination was he tailored for the role of guardian to any young girl, especially this one. He repeated the girl's claim—'that's why my beloved stepmother left you to me in her will'. Strangely put, and surely inverted: *he* was inheriting the girl if anything. The 'beloved' had also rung harsh and false, a curse, not a benediction, that made a nonsense of Mrs Baker's references to her as sweet and shy, and his aunt's labelling her retarded. A fierce demented intelligence had shone in that oddly beautiful face for a moment out of time, but, God help him, part of him wished he had not intruded into her twilight world to witness it. He no longer felt able to walk cleanly away.

CHAPTER TWO

DROPPING the paper-knife he had been shifting from hand to hand with an unaccustomed abstraction, Adam abruptly reached for the telephone and dialled a familiar number. He let it ring and released the breath he had been holding when his mother answered.

'Are you back in London, dear? Did everything go all right?' Nancy enquired pleasantly.

'No to both questions,' Adam replied forcibly. 'Listen, Mother, I need you up here.'

There was a pregnant silence as Mrs Carmichael assimilated Adam's words and tone. It had been over fifteen years since her self-contained son had used the word 'need' to her.

'In Yorkshire?' she asked unnecessarily. 'Why? What's wrong, Adam?'

'Calm down, Mother,' Adam advised, quelling his annoyance at her worried question. Had his mother conveniently forgotten the existence of one Serena Jane Templeton? 'The stepdaughter is proving a problem.' He paused for reaction and when none came he muttered drily, 'That surprise package was rather sprung on me, and I'm not sure how you expect me to handle it.'

'The stepdaughter?' Mrs Carmichael repeated the one phrase that still remained in her head, after having obliterated every other thought. 'Serena?'

'Is there more than one?' Adam returned flippantly, and was instantly contrite as his mother's breathing became discernibly shallower. Perhaps his mother had imagined Serena no longer living with her half-sister and it was a surprise to her too. 'Yes, Mother, Serena Templeton . . . the second husband's daughter.'

'But, Adam, I don't understand. Serena—she's . . .' the faint protest faded completely.

'She's what, Mother?' Adam urged to what seemed like a dead line. 'Are you still there?' He wondered if he should try to reconnect the call.

'Andrea, she told me that . . .' his mother's voice came back, but at half-strength, '. . . just can't believe . . .'

'You can't believe what, Mother?' Adam coaxed gently, now aware of the acute distress at the other end of the line, if not the reason for it. 'Please start making sense, because precious little does round here!'

There was another prolonged silence before Nancy Carmichael spoke again, ignoring his question but with a shade of her normal assurance as she promised to be in Yorkshire as soon as possible.

His mother's vagueness and anxiety did little to make Adam feel easier. Neither did Mr Alexander, arriving after lunch with some palliative literature on a prospective mental home—as if Adam's choice was a foregone conclusion. The solicitor left with an ill-disguised air of satisfaction in spite of the younger man's coldness; in a rare anger Adam tore the brochures up.

And waited.

His mother arrived an hour before dinner in a city taxi-cab with a full complement of suitcases—a complete turnabout from the woman who had declared herself not up to the trip only days before.

Adam gave her a brief kiss on the cheek, before admonishing, 'You should have telephoned. I'd have met you at the station—I've hired a car.'

'There wasn't time before I left London, dear.' Nancy Carmichael recalled the rush that had preceded her journey and Adam noted the strain in her voice.

'Well, I'm glad you decided to come. Do you want to freshen up before dinner?'

'I'd like to see Serena first,' she pressed, sinking down in a chair in the hallway.

'She's resting,' Adam lied—the first thing that came into his head, for from their earlier conversation he had concluded that his mother was as much in the dark about some things as he had been, and right at that moment she did not look ready for any nasty shocks. 'Perhaps later.'

Mrs Baker's appearance in the front hall precluded any further discussion, and after the housekeeper had guided them up to the room she had prepared, he instructed his mother to lie down for a while. It wasn't until they were both seated at the dinner table that the matter which had brought Nancy north was broached.

'Where is Serena?' his mother queried anxiously, after the maid had served the first course. 'I expected to see her at dinner.'

'She has her meals upstairs in splendid isolation,' Adam commented with less than the tact he had intended to use, and his sour tone earned him a sharp glance from his mother.

'How odd, Adam. If I didn't know any better, I would say you and the girl have crossed swords and you've come off worse,' she murmured thoughtfully, and with a thread of amusement asked, 'Is she immune to your fatal charm?'

'I didn't ask you to come up here for a rundown on my character faults, Mother.' Adam was not in the mood for humour, and when he eventually felt his way to enlightening his mother as to the current situation, he doubted she would be either. 'Nor did I make any effort to charm the child.'

'By my reckoning, Serena must be eighteen,' Nancy reflected. 'Hardly a child in this day and age.'

'Well, she's a child as far as I'm concerned,' Adam responded stiffly, and took a long sip of the dry white wine, leaving his soup to grow cold.

'She really has shaken you up.' Nancy Carmichael was surprised at the change in her usually unruffled son. She loved him, but loathed the cool uncaring front he presented to the world. 'It seems that Serena has fulfilled all her early promise to be somebody special.'

Adam groaned inwardly. If special meant what Serena had become, then she was indeed special—but the reappearance of the maid with the main course deprived him off an opportunity to disillusion his mother. Undoubtedly anxious about the girl, yet his mother also seemed to be pleased about something.

'Mother, I'm finding it difficult to understand your attitude,' Adam replied with heavy patience when they were alone again. 'You persuade me to come up to the wilds of Yorkshire to attend your sister's funeral, leaving me in ignorance of the girl's existence and placing me in an extremely awkward situation . . .'

'Actually I didn't realise that Serena would be here,' Nancy interrupted with a rueful grimace.

'Where did you imagine she would be?' Adam asked when a long pause followed the sober statement.

'It's not easy to say.' Nancy fingered the fine string of pearls at her throat, betraying a return to nervousness. 'After the report of the accident—you do know about the accident?'

'Yes. Now,' Adam replied tersely.

'You were away at the time,' she parried the implied criticism. 'Well, anyway, I telephoned and invited Andrea to come to London for a rest and bring the child. We quarrelled rather badly—a misunderstanding.' Nancy Carmichael was always ready to see the best side of anybody's character. 'She accused me of . . . of interfering in her life, and then stunned me with the news that . . . that Serena had died in hospital without regaining consciousness.'

Adam's frown deepened to incredulous shock. 'Have I got this right? Andrea told you the girl was dead?'

'Yes. I know I was at fault, but . . .' Nancy stretched her hands out in a gesture that sought understanding.

'Mother, you're not making sense again,' Adam replied, pushing his plate away. 'How can you be blamed for your sister's incredible lie?'

'Not for the lie as such,' Nancy returned vaguely, 'but I promised Graham I'd look out for her, if anything happened to him.'

'Andrea?' Adam was becoming increasingly lost by his mother's confused narrative.

'No, Serena.' Nancy sensed her son's exasperation. 'I suppose I'd better tell you the whole story.' Her reluctance was evident.'

'Preferably from the beginning, if you can locate it.' Adam softened the sarcasm with a smile, quite prepared to defer his own unpleasant news in the face of his mother's obvious stress.

'I am rambling a bit, aren't I?' Nancy said self-effacingly, returning the squeeze of his fingers. 'It's just that it's all rather upsetting, and Andrea was my sister.'

'Look, Mother, if there are any skeletons in the family closet, then as a fully-paid up member I have the right to hear about them,' he coaxed lightly.

In a rush, Nancy continued, 'Well, as you know, Andrea was many years younger than me. My father married her mother just before the second war. I was in the Wrens when he was killed in an air-raid. Andrea was only eighteen months old when she and her mother were evacuated to Yorkshire. They never returned to London—Clara, my stepmother, couldn't stand the noise of the city any more, even after the bombs had stopped.'

Adam supposed this family history was leading somewhere, although quite where he couldn't see.

'And?' he prompted.

'We lost touch, I'm afraid, and then about seven years ago, when we ran into each other in London, I invited her to stay for a while—I hoped we might develop a closer relationship, even after all those years of silence,' Nancy murmured quietly, her tone giving the impression that things had not turned out as planned. 'We met Graham at a garden party—such a nice man! He'd just come back from Italy with his little girl. His wife had died a few years earlier and he felt he owed Serena a better upbringing than he could provide in a small fishing village. Like most artists he tended to be forgetful of worldly things and Serena had begun to run a little wild. Not that she wasn't a very lovable child,' Nancy hastened to emphasise, 'always asking questions and sparklingly alive, although not at all precocious.'

Serena, as a young child, had certainly impressed people favourably. Adam wondered what his mother would make of the pathetic creature she had become.

'And so they fell in love and got married?' he suggested with more than a touch of sardonicism.

'Not exactly.' Nancy appeared remote, involved in the past. 'They did get on well, and Andrea could be most pleasant and charming. The child needed a stable home and a mother, and Andrea seemed both willing and able to fit the role perfectly. Graham was looking for security for the child, and to a certain extent for himself. Not financial, of course.'

'Of course,' Adam mocked. Graham Templeton hadn't exactly lost out by it all. 'This house is a far cry from the traditional artist's garret,' he pointed out dryly. 'A very practical arrangement.'

'I don't think you yourself are a great believer in romantic love, so you can hardly blame him,' Nancy defended. She had liked Graham Templeton and his young daughter. 'He was in his late forties at the time and he thought he was acting for the best—an arrangement that would suit them all.'

'Only it didn't work out that way,' Adam mused as a certain painting came to mind.

'I . . , I don't know,' she said with a distinct hesitation.

'"Hear no evil, speak no evil, see no evil,"' he softly taunted his mother's philosophy.

'Who can tell what goes on inside a marriage?' Nancy evaded his searching gaze and concentrated on neatly folding her linen napkin.

'Why didn't you tell me all this before?' he asked accusingly.

'Well, you were abroad most of that time, and you've never really shown any interest in family gossip,' she parried.

And his mother hated discussing the unpleasant—a virtue in most cases, but it made it more difficult for Adam in the current circumstances.

'Shall we move to the lounge for coffee?' he suggested. 'I have *some* news for you.'

Later, when the coffee had been poured, Adam remarked conversationally, 'I found some paintings of Templeton's in a studio at the back of the house. There's a rather good portrait of Andrea.'

For good, Nancy read pleasant to look at, and affirmed, 'Yes, she was a very good-looking woman. She took after our father.' She tilted her head to one side and looked consideringly at Adam before continuing, 'You have a likeness to him too—around the eyes.'

'I can't say I'd noticed,' Adam said uninterestedly.

'Perhaps Andrea had, that time you met, remember. And that's why she wanted you to have the house,' Nancy said thoughtfully.

'Sentimental rubbish, Mother,' Adam derided without any real maliciousness, and then realising just what his mother had said, he pressed, 'You *knew* that I was to inherit her estate?'

'I suspected so, yes,' Nancy confirmed, and when her son sighed heavily she admitted, 'I suppose I should have told you, but her letter was a little strange. She was ill, but she didn't want to see me, and if anything happened to her, she would like *you* to take care of her personal effects.' Her expression clouded over with the remembered hurt.

'Such as an eighteen-year-old child,' he uttered aloud.

'I'm so looking forward to seeing her again,' Nancy enthused. 'Despite the shock of your news, I'm dying to find out all about her.'

'Well, she's special, just as you imagined,' he said grimly.

He set his coffee cup firmly down on the table but was conscious that he was now deferring the unpleasant as he asked, 'So why did Andrea lie to you about the girl?'

'I don't really know,' Nancy shrugged. 'Does any of it really matter now?'

'Mustn't speak ill of the dead, eh?' he chivvied before rising to cross over to the drinks cabinet, and pouring them both a brandy. 'Well, it just might be relevant when we come to decide what's to be done about Serena.'

'Was she frightfully dependent on Andrea?' his mother asked anxiously as she took the glass Adam was holding out to her.

'You could say that,' he muttered, resuming his seat and finishing his brandy in one gulp. But just as he was reaching the conclusion that there was no way to dress up the truth, his mother gave a decisive nod and started outlining plans in a gentle monotone.

'The way I see it, there are two things we could do, but it's really up to Serena. When she's feeling a little better, that is. She can come back to London with me. I'd like that, myself, and she could do the debutante scene for a year until she meets someone suitable. Or she could go to a finishing school—perhaps that would be better.'

Adam's laughter cut rudely into her suggestions, and it earned him a look of total disdain from his mother. Why must he always treat every matter with such careless levity?

'Really, Adam, I hoped you could at least take this seriously—it is another person's future we're discussing!'

'I'm sorry, Mother, my laughter was ironic rather than humorous,' he excused himself, his mouth now a straight line. 'I'm certain the girl upstairs wouldn't welcome or be welcomed in a finishing school for young ladies.'

'Why? She's not . . .' Nancy searched for the most delicate word and finished with, 'fast, is she?'

'No, Serena is definitely a virgin,' he replied, making no concession to conversational niceties. 'She looks about fourteen and it's highly unlikely she's had any contact with the opposite sex.' It was coming out badly, but he had to say it now he had started. 'She's autistic,' he finished, settling for the most clinical word he could find.

'Autistic?' Nancy echoed in her bafflement.

'Autistic, withdrawn, bats in the belfry. I don't know the exact diagnosis,' he expanded brutally.

'How can you say a thing like that?' Nancy glared at her son lounging with apparent casualness, his long legs stretched out in front of him. 'Is this one of your cruel, sophisticated jokes, because if it is . . .'

'You malign me, Mother,' Adam interrupted briskly, getting through to her with an unequivocal, 'No, this is no joke. I wish it was. Since the accident, the girl has become increasingly morose, verging on the autistic.' An image of the girl staring at rather than through her window came to mind, as he added, 'She's cut off from reality, absorbed in her own thought processes. I got a few words out of her, none of them making much sense.'

'Oh, dear God!' Nancy groaned her reaction, closing her eyes as though she could shut out what he was telling her. 'I should have checked, should have sensed Andrea was lying.'

Adam moved to the empty sofa space next to his mother and put a comforting arm around her, but his tone was firm.

'Mother, there's absolutely no reason for you to take any guilt for the girl's condition on yourself. The accident left her unhinged; it's that simple.'

'Perhaps it is,' Nancy moaned, shaking her head distressfully from side to side, 'but I promised Graham, and I let him down.'

'Why did Templeton ask you to look out for the girl?' Adam asked quietly, needing to test a nagging doubt. 'Did the relationship between Andrea and her stepdaughter deteriorate when they were under the same roof?'

'Oh, no, nothing like that,' Nancy denied at once. 'I'm sure Graham simply wanted me to help Andrea if anything happened to him. She wasn't used to children, you see.' She paused reflectively before continuing, 'Perhaps Andrea resented the idea of interference after the tragedy, but she was always very kind to Serena. A bit over-anxious at times, but that was understandable. She so much wanted Serena to accept her almost as a mother.'

'And they lived happily ever after,' Adam quoted sarcastically as another image arose of the pale ghost the girl had faded into. 'Only they didn't.'

'The accident,' Nancy reminded him, but Adam threw her an oblique glance that told her she wasn't fooling anybody. 'All right, there was some tension, but it didn't involve Serena. I came once to the house after the marriage, at Graham's invitation, but Andrea didn't make me feel welcome. They were both trying too hard. Andrea wanted more than Graham was capable of giving her. While she was looking for the romantic love that I don't think existed in her first marriage, Graham couldn't feel more than deep affection. Serena's real mother was a very beautiful, captivating girl and he was still emotionally involved with her memory.'

'The man was a fool to remarry,' Adam condemned.

'Adam! Sometimes I think you're totally without compassion,' Nancy countered, shocked and hurt by his cutting comment. 'Nobody is infallible or capable of predicting the outcome of their actions.'

'I don't believe that, Mother. Man is able to control his life, his destiny,' he espoused his own brand of philosophy.

'He used the idea of fatalism as an excuse for his own failing, that's all.'

'And what about love?' Nancy challenged softly, disturbed by Adam's hard creed. 'What would happen, Adam, if you fell in love and your feelings weren't returned? You couldn't have that woman and nothing you could do would change things? How could you control *that* situation?'

Adam slipped his arm from his mother's shoulders. 'Do all women think the world is well lost for love?' he sighed heavily, before moving away to pour himself another drink. This topic of conversation had been coming a long time, but this was not the moment to choose for a heart-to-heart! He didn't want to hurt her, but he had to make it clear and unequivocal.

'Mother, I'm thirty-five years old, and as I've escaped this dreaded affliction up until now, I see no reason why I should ever succumb. If I desire a woman, I send her flowers and tell her she's the most fascinating woman in the world, which of course is true for me at the time, but I don't need to call it love to justify the relationship.'

His mother was appalled by his cynicism, carved in every well-defined angle of his haughty, handsome face. 'I loved your father—I still do.'

'I know that, Mother.' He heard the catch in her voice and softened perceptibly. 'But that sort of love is very rare—almost extinct. It can't exist in a world that's becoming increasingly brutalised.'

'I don't understand you, Adam,' she said, shaking her head despairingly.

He looked down on her beautifully arranged white hair and the blue eyes that seemed to retain all the innocence of childhood, a remarkable feat for a woman past her sixieth birthday. She belonged to a different age. He felt enough had been said on the subject and they were in grave danger of quarrelling for the first time in twenty years. He yawned deliberately.

'I'm exhausted. Coming up?'

He stretched out a hand to help his mother up and resignedly Nancy Carmichael took it. She had been wasting her breath, and now she felt very tired. Sometimes Adam made it very difficult for her to keep believing in him as any more than one of the unscrupulous pack with whom he loosely ran.

As they climbed the stairs together, her thoughts returned to Serena. How she hoped that for once, his clinically exact way with words would prove inaccurate!

Their voices, quiet and conversational as they both made an effort to draw back from the earlier hostility, reached Serena as faint whispers that held menace to a mind that was absorbed by dreams of past and prone to vivid imagining that protected itself from unacceptable reality. But with his intrusion Adam had somehow made it through the barriers and established himself as a force in her life, although her image of him was distorted by her growing problem with distinguishing fantasy and fact.

His faint resemblance to his aunt had a more sinister impact on a girl who had been pierced by penetrating grey eyes of the exact same shade.

'I want to help you,' he had said, and she had heard the words and the sincerity behind them, but they brought back echoes of a thousand broken promises.

'Come on, Serena, we'll be friends.' And hours, or minutes or perhaps even seconds later, the bitter ranting would start all over. And then the pendulum would swing once more. 'You're my little girl now, and I'll look after you. I love you.'

And the mark of Andrea's affection would stand scarlet on Serena's pale cheekbone. Miraculously she had come through, survived Andrea. The key was to lose fear, cease caring about the present. But there were penalties for the tricks she had learned. She was slipping away from it all. Too far to come back now.

CHAPTER THREE

SLEEP eluded him. It was this damn country quiet. The rain had at last stopped and the hush was such that he could distinguish individual sounds, and the water dripping from the roof guttering was sending him crazy. He grimaced at the unfortunate choice of words before slipping out of bed and scanning the wardrobe for a bathrobe.

He left the house shrouded in darkness as he felt his way downstairs and crossed the hall to the library. His aunt's collection of books was large and varied, row upon row of hardbacks in mint condition that suggested they were there as a showpiece. There were even several of his own novels. He had never read any of his own writing after it appeared in print and he wasn't about to break the habit now; instead he chose a political thriller.

A board at the top of the stairs creaked and Adam almost passed off that other noise as a similar complaint from a very old house. But he delayed long enough to catch it again, coming from the corridor that lay on the left of the wide staircase and growing louder as he stood and listened for it. Slowly pacing the passageway, he homed in on it.

Curtains open, the moonlight streamed into the girl's room and clearly outlined the huddled form, shivering and emitting low fitful whimpers. Hesitatingly he came forward to rearrange the bedclothes that had slipped to the uncarpeted floor and tucked the blankets loosely round Serena's small frame. Her trembling did not cease. The room was like an icebox, but beads of sweat glistened on her forehead. Gripped in bad dreams, she began to toss from side to side, once more dislodging her covers.

Adam crossed to the washhand basin in the far corner

and ran a facecloth under the cold tap. Treading lightly, he eased himself down on the bed, careful not to wake the sleeping girl, and gently wiped her face and neck. He hoped to soothe her out of the nightmare, but the movements became more frantic, her breathing more laboured, until the girl erupted into wakefulness.

Dream merged into reality with the dark shadowed face that loomed threateningly over her, and she let out a full-blooded scream. Pure instinct drove him to clamp a hard hand over her mouth to stifle the sharp cry, but it was just as quickly removed when small, incisive teeth bit viciously into the fleshy part of his palm, just below the fingers. Fists rained blows on his bare chest where the borrowed robe had parted, and several seconds passed before he reacted on her startling show of latent strength. He managed to capture one wrist, but she continued to hit out with her free hand. An expression of fear had given way to a fierce, burning anger in the vivid green eyes. When a well-aimed blow hit him squarely in the eye he ceased merely trying to restrain her and took positive action, gripping her shoulders and leaning forward to trap her upper body beneath his weight.

Suddenly she went quite still. Faces bare inches apart, their stares locked. Adam felt a flicker of incongruous triumph as a look of submission entered her eyes. He slackened off his hold and swore silently at his simplicity as a knee landed hard on his hipbone. Making a desperate grab for her before she could start again, he accidentally caught her cotton nightdress, and as she continued struggling wildly, the much-washed material rent in two.

Her white breasts, small but perfectly formed, rose and fell as she lay, hair splayed on the pillow, trying to get her breath back to resume the fight. Adam was unable to stop himself staring at their movement, and disgust within himself fought a sweet fascination. Her skin was like alabaster, a living sculpture in the half-light, and he wanted to touch its smoothness. A low moan of desire unconsciously escaped his lips, and he made a move to cover her. It was her violent attempt to push him away that made him lose his balance, brought his flesh against hers and effectively knocked the wind out of her. But it was Adam who was a fraction too slow to lift his body away, and despite her youth and innocence, she recognised the betrayal of his wanting as their eyes met once more.

Seconds ticked by—a suspension of hostility as each tried to come to terms with the shift in emotion. And then a cry of sheer terror was vibrating the air, acting like a cold shower on Adam's heightened senses. God, he thought, the girl believed he was going to rape her! It was like a scene from a bad play, and now too late to rewrite his part. In desperation he moved her head back to face him, forcing her to read his expression.

'Look, Serena, I'm not going to hurt you.'

The girl was oblivious to the tenderness in his voice, to the silent pleading of his dark eyes, as her cries, mingled with choking sobs, became louder, more frenzied, till he was scared for her and felt ineffectual in the face of the demons that were driving her on.

'In God's name, what have you done?' Nancy Carmichael stood in the doorway, rigid with shock, as she snapped on the light and took in the whole scene, damning to her son in every detail.

Backing off the bed, Adam turned to look at his mother, but almost immediately his eyes were pulled back to Serena. He had become part of the nightmare that had landed him in this situation.

The girl's heartrending sobs, somewhat muffled by the pillow in which she had buried her head, forced Nancy Carmichael into action. Brushing past Adam, she gathered the girl in her arms, gently rocking and soothing much as she would a crying toddler. After an initial attempt to shove the older woman away, Serena collapsed into the warm protective embrace, her crying eventually subsiding to a whimper.

'I didn't mean to hurt her in any way.' The hands that raked through Adam's hair were shaking. He was having a hard time believing it had all happened.

Feeling the girl's tremor of fear at the harsh, male tone Nancy rapped out,' Get out, Adam. Now!'

For a lifetime he would remember the look on the pale tear-stained face that rested on his mother's shoulder—the look of intense fear. There was nothing he could do about it—he had put it there.

'Hush now, my lamb, I'll look after you.'

Nancy Carmichael was as good as her word; she stayed until the girl exhausted herself into sleep and held her all the while. And Serena, who had no real idea of the identity of her comforter, nevertheless accepted her, for she smelt of flowers and brought back the memory of a beautiful mother to whose soft skin had always clung the smell of violet or rose.

The mirror told Adam he looked forty; he felt even older. His eyes were shot with blood, the left one underlined by the shadow of a bruise. A day's growth of dark stubble completed the disreputable picture.

Showered and shaved, he admitted to an improvement, but his head was still fragile, the loud knocking doing nothing to alleviate the pain.

'Yes?' he barked.

'It's me!' his mother called through the closed door.

He groaned silently, but the meeting was inevitable. 'Come in.' He finished buttoning up the front of a freshly-laundered shirt and reached for his tie.

For a long moment they faced each other as wary strangers, until his mother broke the disturbing atmosphere by stating the obvious, 'You look ghastly.'

'I feel worse,' Adam muttered, concentrating on knotting his tie. 'But I don't suppose you've come to discuss my state of health.'

'No, I've not,' she said primly. 'Especially as your illness is self-inflicted.'

'And I'm equally sure you're not here to deliver a temperance sermon, Mother.' He hadn't meant to resort to flippancy, but he felt irritatingly defensive.' How did you know I'd been having a drink?'

'More than one, I should say, from the empty bottle of brandy I found lying on the living room floor.' Her voice was heavy with disapproval; she was determined not to be disarmed by him.

'I'm a big boy now, Mother,' he murmured dryly as he crossed to the dressing table and used one of the brushes lying there.

Nancy knew if she didn't challenged him outright, her questions would go unanswered. 'I want to know about last night, Adam.'

Their eyes made brief contact in the mirror glass.

'Is there any point?' His tone was resigned.

'Of course there is!' she exclaimed, and stepping forward, continued rashly, 'You can't do what you did and not expect to be asked to explain your actions!'

It brought Adam spinning round, dropping any interest in his appearance. 'And what is it exactly I'm supposed to have done?'

Nancy became flustered; she had not intended making accusations. 'I'm trying to be fair, Adam.' She spread her hands in an appeal for reasonableness. 'Trying to understand.'

'Innocent until proved guilty, eh? But I suspect our little princess has already given her version with every sordid detail.'

'Why do you call Serena that?' his mother asked, alarmed by his bitterness.

'No reason. Forget it.' Last night he had felt utter self-loathing, but with the morning, his emotion had taken on a different complexion. He had not realised how strongly he felt towards the girl until the words were out, and it was difficult to analyse the change in attitude—resentment was the nearest he could get to pinning it down.

'Actually, I haven't seen Serena this morning, and she didn't utter one word after you left her room,' Nancy declared, resting her tired weight down on the edge of the bed.

'So I've got a reprieve,' he responded with mock relief.

'I'm not going to have a duel of words with you, Adam. Anything you care to tell me, I shall believe.' She knew her son was not a liar.

Adam picked up a packet of cigarettes from his bedside table and lit one before replying staccato-like,' All right, Mother. Serena was having a nightmare. I heard her crying. I went to see if I could calm her down, and I startled her.'

'And?' Nancy prompted softly.

'End of story,' Adam clipped out.

'And that's why she was screaming the house down?' Nancy commented, adopting some of her son's dryness.

'I don't think she likes me very much.' He smiled crookedly. The understatement of the year!

'Did you . . . did you try to seduce her?' She felt rather foolish asking this, for despite the evidence of her own eyes, in the cold light of day the idea seemed ludicrous.

'No—no, I didn't.' His denial was slow to come. She waited for him to continue, knowing there was more. The admission was forced out of him. 'But I wanted to.'

'Adam, how could you?' Nancy gasped, not ready for the truth now it had been given to her. She protested, 'She's just a child, like you said.'

'I don't know, Mother.' Last night came back to him with total clarity, although he had tried to erase it with the drink he had later consumed. 'I wish I did. She woke up when I was wiping the perspiration from her face, and then she was attacking me, as though I was something bad out of her nightmare.'

Nancy shut her eyes wearily for a moment before saying tentatively, 'Adam, I've got to ask. Did you . . . did you touch her in any way?'

'No!' He was angry, mostly because her question, delicately put, called up a memory of the girl's satin-white body, and the almost overwhelming desire he had had to trail his fingers across the soft pure skin. 'What do you take me for?'

'A human being, with all the fallibilities that entails.' And right at that moment, although he was giving little away verbally, his drawn features made him appear intensely human. 'She's too young for you, even if . . . Too delicate.'

She was warning him off, and it infuriated him that she should think it necessary. 'A moment's craziness doesn't constitute a desire to conduct a full-blown affair, Mother.'

He was angry, far too angry about it all, but Nancy replied quietly, 'Good.' Her response lacked conviction.

'God, Mother, her top ripped in the struggle to calm her, her breasts were bare, and I wanted to make love to her for a couple of seconds. But not her—any faceless, nameless girl in the same set of circumstances.' Nancy had been wrong; Adam was capable of lying to her, but it did not work on himself. He crushed his cigarette out. 'Unfortunately she misinterpreted my intentions and thought I was about to rape her. For that, I'm sorry, but in broad daylight I have about as much interest in that skinny, nutty kid as I have in the little parlourmaid!'

She had not heard her son so vehement about anything for many years, and in a different situation it might have pleased her that he had lost that air of nonchalance that made him seem such a cold uncaring individual.

'What are we going to do about the child?' she queried anxiously, deciding to close the subject of last night.

'What are *you* going to do about her, you mean.' Adam strode to the tallboy and whipped out his suit jacket. 'I'm going back to London in the hire car, and if I ever have to come back to this morgue,' he growled, his gesture taking in the house, 'or have to meet that crazy girl again, it will be too soon! Do what you like with her. I just don't care—as long as you keep her well away from me. She's bad news as far as I'm concerned!'

Nancy was unsure how much he really meant, since her son must know she wouldn't abandon Serena.

'You can become her guardian, as per the terms of the will, but I'll be very happy to look after her,' she returned quietly, and mitigated his pitiless assertions with, 'And I think it's probably a good idea for you to stay away for a while until she's a little better . . . until she's ready to face the world again.'

God help it, he muttered to himself in reply to his mother's optimism, but some of the anger was draining from him, leaving him to wonder more rationally at its source. He should have been able to laugh at his mother's insinuations, or at least shrug them off.

'You'll stay to lunch?'

Adam hardened himself to the plea in her voice. 'No, I've got to get back. I promised to take Julia out this evening.' A small fabrication, since he doubted he would relish Julia's company in his present mood.

'Take care.' Months went by often when they didn't see each other, but this had the atmosphere of a real parting. Nancy Carmichael was close to tears; she felt, however ridiculous, that he had put her in the position of choosing between him and the girl. She reached out and tentatively touched his arm. 'Don't turn your back on us, Adam.'

He stiffened, but responded with forced lightness, 'I'll see you when you come down to London. Don't bury yourself up here.'

'I don't see it that way. Looking after Serena will give me something worthwhile to do with my life.'

'The grandchild I never gave you?' he suggested, and smiled, although he had never felt less like doing so when he saw the suspicion of tears in her ageless eyes.

'Yes, perhaps,' she admitted, and returned his smile.

'Come on.' He picked his keys and wallet off the bedside table and curved his arm round her shoulders. 'See me down to the car.'

They walked slowly down the stairs, not saying much, and emerged into bright sunlight that stole some of the bleakness from the environment. Adam appeared perfectly relaxed as he unlocked the car, slipped out of his suit jacket and tossed it carelessly in the back seat, but when he straightened and his eyes drifted upwards to the second storey, he knew he was running rather than walking away.

A small face unflinchingly returned his stare. In all likelihood she was looking through, not at him, but he imagined it to be accusing him of cowardice.

He spun round and gripped his mother's arms, not conscious of the pressure he was exerting in his sudden urgency. 'Listen, Mother, you get a psychiatrist for that kid. Today. Now!' His voice was almost a growl as he read the doubt flickering in her eyes. 'It's no kindness to pretend she's normal. She isn't. And whatever reason Andrea had for locking her up in her ivory tower, I don't think it was kindness.'

'I—I'm not sure I understand,' Nancy stammered her bewilderment at the change in her son's attitude.

He couldn't explain—it wasn't much more than an impression of something sinister about the whole set-up. 'Just get someone in straight away.'

He was gone within seconds of receiving her promise, but he had left his sense of urgency, and Nancy, flicking through her sister's telephone book, dialled the family doctor. The first stage had begun.

She cried the first month—about nothing, about everything. She remembered a pinpoint light in her eyes and a voice that said, 'She's had some sort of cathartic shock, probably her stepmother's death, but she's definitely back with us,' and a silver-haired woman smiling towards her.

But Serena wished she wasn't; she wanted to return to the shadows of the distant past. 'I've got a friend,' the voice continued, 'he's over at St Thomas's . . .'

And later another voice. But this one seemed younger and didn't wear tweed or smell of pipe tobacco. He couldn't be a doctor, could he?

'Call me Simon,' the voice had said, sitting next to her at the window after the others had left them alone.

And despite five years out of the world, Serena recognised the nature of the man. 'You're not wearing a white coat,' she accused, when he talked on in a reassuring tone, undaunted by her refusal to acknowledge him.

'Should I be?' he asked mildly.

'Yes, I think so,' she replied thoughtfully, and recalling a song that had been playing on the radio one summer her parents had taken her on a visit back to England, she said with a tinge of mischief, 'They're coming to take me away—the little men in their little white coats.'

She had meant to make him laugh, show him she didn't need him, but instead he had stared silently back at her. And Serena imagined he was thinking, 'The girl's crazy!' For a while she slipped back into her safe, fantasy world. But it was getting harder all the time now to hold on to her father. She had to force him to come back to her, and he went so easily, at the slightest sound or movement.

Happy in her work, Lizzie was dusting in time to the music on the radiogram. The new mistress had certainly brought changes to this room. The furniture was still old-fashioned, not like the pieces she admired in the big stores in Leeds, but it no longer gave you backache just looking at it. Yes, everything was bright under Mrs Carmichael who actually saw you as a human being. Well, maybe not everything. The old lady might have managed to get the girl downstairs, but where was the improvement if she simply stared at the fire instead of her bedroom window?

Lizzie finished the photographs on the mantelpiece, sighing over the son's. He was a dark one all right, disappearing after his second day up here and then off to America, without even coming up to say goodbye to his mother. Perhaps Mrs Baker was right—handsome is as handsome does—but she nevertheless gave his picture an extra rub, before turning up the music and moving on to the display cabinet at the far end of the room.

She was busy on a Dresden shepherdess when she realised she was suddenly singing unaccompanied. They both looked surprised—the girl with her finger on the radio dial and the maid slowly rising from her knees. 'You switched it off,' became 'she switched it off', as Lizzie snapped out of her daze and raced out of the living room.

The noise had grown louder and louder, till Serena couldn't bring one memory back in her head, and a surge of anger made her move to the source of the voice wailing in the background. But the peace had been momentary. She could hear Lizzie out in the hall announcing her action at the top of her voice, and was struck by the absurdity of it. She was nineteen years old and a miracle was being proclaimed because she had turned off a radio. It was funny. She sat down and cried.

Nancy Carmichael hushed the excited Lizzie and steeled herself for disappointment when she entered the room. In two months, the progress had been slight, so slight it could have been imagined. She was crying again, and although Simon Clark, the psychiatrist, said it was a good sign, Nancy felt crushed by the sight of enormous, soundless tears spurting from the girl's unblinking eyes.

The moment Nancy sat down on the sofa beside the girl and touched her shoulder, she knew there was a change. For the first time Serena went voluntarily into her arms for the comfort she had provided over the last few weeks, and when the crying stopped, she did not retreat from her.

'Am I mentally ill?' Serena asked starkly.

Whatever Nancy had been expecting, it wasn't that

sharp agonised question, and she visibly floundered.
Tear-washed, tormented eyes were waiting for her
answer, and it was on the tip of her tongue to say, 'Of
course not, dear', but she was caught by Adam's warnings, repeated in the letter he had sent before leaving
England.

'You have been sick, but you're getting better, aren't
you?' Nancy smiled reassuringly, and prayed she had said
the right thing.

Serena concentrated on that thought. If she was getting
better, why did she feel unhappier than she had for years?
But this woman hadn't lied to her. She had held her and
stroked her hair when the misery began to choke her, and
she had asked for nothing back.

'I've forgotten who you are,' Serena muttered
ashamedly.

'I'm your . . .' Nancy checked herself, since the loss of
her stepmother might still be a source of pain, and said
instead, 'I'm an old friend of your father's.'

'Did he send you?'

'Yes. Yes, he did, dear,' Nancy recalled, although so
many years had passed and she had arrived late. But not
too late, Nancy was suddenly sure.

'That's why he doesn't need to come any more,' Serena
remarked solemnly, then wished she hadn't, because the
woman was looking at her the same way call-me-Simon
did. She wanted to give her something back for all she had
taken. 'I used to dream about him in my head. Just
dreams. I know they're not real.'

'No, dear, but dreams are nice.' Nancy pushed the hair
back from Serena's face and saw a glimmer of the child she
had been. 'They help us get through the bad times when
we lose someone we love.'

They weren't just words. The woman knew. 'I miss him
so,' Serena whispered, and the tears started again, only
they were the tears of a young girl, noisy and resoundingly
natural.

CHAPTER FOUR

HE was 'stoned'. It was a good word, Adam decided. One of the Americanisms that had filtered into his vocabulary over the last twelve months, it captured perfectly his state of calm reserved intoxication. There was no danger of his falling off his high bar-stool, or making a drunken pass at one of the beautiful women who came in line for his lazy inspection, or even slurring the precise well-modulated speech that pronounced him so British. Nevertheless he had consumed enough Bourbon to render him partially immune.

He was at a party—where or whose he couldn't quite remember, but that didn't worry him unduly; there were parties every night of the week in Beverly Hills—an endless variety of parties that ranged from the bizarre to the mindlessly dull. They were Julia's natural element, gave her a setting for her flamboyant night-time beauty, and allowed her to indulge in her single-minded passion for dressing up. And as for Adam—well, he accompanied Julia to whatever social function she had wangled an invitation to and played his part as the satirical half of that charming English couple who were popular newcomers to the movie world.

The glitter of Hollywood that had been sufficient to amuse Adam in its social observance for a limited period had now completely tarnished and the inclination to laugh at it all had largely deserted him. Yet he was still religiously attending these affairs—Julia's faithful follower. That image brought a crooked smile to his lips—even she wasn't fooled. Adam had changed, but not that much. He arrived and left with Julia, but the hours that spaced the two events rarely brought them into contact. And he wasn't fooling himself either, he realised, as he lifted the glass to his lips—the party round was, for him, a socially acceptable periphery for his steady studious drinking.

He checked the gold watch on his wrist and was mildly surprised as it was early by Hollywood standards and yet Julia was slowly manoeuvring her way towards him, exchanging flirtatious remarks with the men she thought it worth cultivating and light, meaningless flattery with the women she couldn't afford to snub. Adam had to give her her due—she had carved herself a much higher niche than was warranted by her tenuous association with the film world through a writer.

'Shall I call a taxi?' Adam spared her a sideways glance that picked up her unpleasant mood, now that her back was turned on the other occupants of the room.

'Taxi?' She allowed a perplexed frown to wrinkle her smooth forehead for a brief moment before deciding to ignore his incomprehensible remark. 'Adam, I think you should circulate. People are beginning to talk.'

As far as Adam could tell from the rabble that had penetrated his hazy indifference, the people to whom she was referring hadn't *stopped* doing just that since the party had started. He didn't air his cynicism but confined himself to a relatively innocuous, 'Why?'

Julia's fingers tightened on the edge of the bar counter. 'Sometimes, Adam, you can be damned impossible!' she countered waspishly.

He caught her dramatically made up eyes moving from the Bourbon bottle back to his face and raised a mocking eyebrow in mild challenge.

'Join me? Or have you come to save my soul from the demon drink?' he taunted softly, knowing no such idea was in her mind. 'The love of a *good* woman and all that.'

'As far as I'm concerned . . . darling,' she changed from petulance to saccharine sweetness when another guest moved within earshot, 'you can drink as much as you like.' It made him more manageable, usually.

'That's what I thought, darling,' he mimicked her endearment and was awarded a look of utter dislike for his trouble.

'I don't ask much of you, Adam,' she announced, reverting to one of her favourite roles of the long-suffering injured partner.

There had to be an answer for that! But Adam did not choose to follow it up; there was no point in their carving each other up, and besides, he didn't care enough to bother.

'But I think the least you can do is play host at our own party,' she finished tautly.

A lazy smile spread over Adam's still good-looking face as he surveyed the split-level room, bounded by much tinted glass and housing a collection of expensive nondescript furniture and a plethora of trendy Mexican artifacts supposedly present to lend individuality; and the smile of dawning awareness evolved into laughter as he focused on a grotesque figurehead that had come with the rest of the fittings when he had leased the house. He sincerely hoped there weren't two like it!

He was saved from giving an explanation for his sudden amusement, for Julia, having delivered a less than lady-like expletive, was already stalking away, undoubtedly rearranging her party smile as she moved towards the terrace that fronted the mandatory swimming-pool.

'Wow! That's some lady!' The remark was accompanied by a low, appreciative whistle from the guest now seated along from Adam, but when neither received a similar male response, the American added apologetically, 'Your wife?'

'Just good friends,' Adam responded with heavy irony, and joined in the other's laughter when his comment was obviously misinterpreted. But he had no desire for idle conversation, and downing his drink, moved away to his study at the front of the mini-mansion. Cut off from the main living quarters, it was his sanctuary from the steady stream of callers that invaded the house during daylight hours. It was where he did his work, such as it was.

Originally he had been contracted by Hamlisch Studios to adapt one of his own novels for the screen; the idea had originated from one of its directors a good year before he had taken it up, and the arrangements had been made by telephone; ready for change and fresh out from England, Adam found that project had gone reasonably well, and he had completed the screenplay within the first three months.

But he had stayed on to write directly for films, and that had been a big mistake. Too independently wealthy to feel pressure at the idea of being under a reviewable contract, nevertheless he had been badly influenced in his writing by his disaffection with the whole circus. Times when he returned from the studio after a meeting with a producer who punctuated every sentence with the byword 'commercial', and a devil in him prompted him to pen screeds of highly sensational garbage, and the same black humour was satisfied when it was greeted with enthusiasm instead of the scorn he thought it so richly deserved. He wasn't doing much for his reputation and he knew it, but he was hooked on self-destruction. And he knew that too.

The study was the only room in this screamingly modern house that held any impression of Adam—a crate's worth of books shipped from London, his collection of classical and blues records—and a painting that he had brought thousands of miles, treated like a priceless Rembrandt in transit and then found mostly he couldn't bear to look at, although it remained where it had first been hung, between two garish abstracts.

He poured himself another drink. There was a cocktail cabinet in every room—an absurd but convenient status symbol. He sat down at a desk littered with a week's unopened mail and sorted through it—mostly bills that Julia had carelessly run up. Julia who never asked for much. True enough, he supposed. She never *asked*, and he met her extravagances without comment.

The letter with the Yorkshire postmark he left till last, like an anticipated pleasure, or maybe bad news postponed. From its bulk, it was not one of his mother's regular monthly letters. This would be the third psychiatrist's report she had sent him, taking his guardianship seriously.

The first had been brief, couched in jargon which, translated, came down to the fact that Serena Templeton was extremely and unhealthily withdrawn, which hadn't been anything Adam hadn't already known. The second, a summary of six months' treatment, had been cautiously optimistic, referring to an increasing response from the patient when quizzed on completely impersonal matters or incidents relating to her early life in Italy but an avoidance of any discussion on the years that had followed.

He wished his mother wouldn't send them: he experienced a curious excitement when he began to read them, but was left with a profound dissatisfaction that lingered for days. Neither emotion he fully understood or appreciated.

Sobered, his eyes moved rapidly over the neatly typed pages and then went back over the key sentences.

'I have been treating the patient for fourteen months, and the transition from a morose, wary shadow to a lovely, vital young woman is nothing short of miraculous. However, from a scientific viewpoint, I am extremely suspicious of miracles. On the surface Serena appears quite ready to "fly solo" as she herself has expressed it, but I have reservations. Not once in the long hours of analysis have I been able to identify the source of her illness. The effects were clearly visible, the causes have remained her jealously-guarded secret.

'What is also disturbing is her ability to sense my reluctance and her reaction to it. Recently she asked me directly if she wasn't allowed to be given her "sanity certificate" until she had undergone the ritual purging of her soul, proceeded to trot out some implausible fantasies relating to her stepmother, and then laughed in the face of my refusal to play a part in her charade.

'Since this conversation, I have made no further progress. Cases like Serena's, where the patient is intelligent and highly intuitive, tend to be problematic, for she pre-guesses where my questions are leading and chooses whether she wished to go there or lead me round in polite circles. Despite this impasse, I recommend that treatment continues and she does not try out her newly-found "wings" yet.'

Adam discerned from the tone of the report that the psychiatrist was deeply involved with his case, not withstanding Serena's lack of co-operation. Recalling his own abortive attempt to help her, Adam sympathised with the man's evident frustration. And he too did not believe in miracles outside the context of the Old and New Testaments, although from earlier letters his mother obviously did. He turned to her accompanying note.

'Dear Adam,

'I have enclosed Simon Clark's report for you to read and give me your impartial advice, but I wish you to bear in mind my own impressions.

'I know that in ways I'm a naïve old woman, but Serena is now, to my eyes, every inch the beautiful bright girl she promised to be as a child. I wish you could see her, Adam. It's hard to believe she was ill at all. Sometimes she herself is so rational about it all, she reminds me of you and your calm practical approach to life.

'She spends much of her time painting and seems to have inherited her father's talent, although frankly some of her work is incomprehensible to me. However, she needs formal training, and with that in mind, we submitted a portfolio of sketches to the Art College in Leeds, and on the strength of her promise, they were willing to give her a place in September without the usual academic requirements.

'I realise it was foolish of me to act without first consulting Simon, and he is, as you will gather from his report, opposed to the idea of subjecting her to any stress, but it's hard to stand against Serena's quiet certainty that she can cope.

'So where do I go from here? I told Serena I would write to you, and since then she hasn't mentioned the subject. It's as though she's making herself resigned to not going, and it's this very mature acceptance itself that gives me faith in her.

'As for Simon, he undoubtedly deserves the fine reputation he has gained for such a young man and is very devoted to Serena's interest, coming frequently to visit her, but I do not feel his attitude is strictly analytical. I believe Serena is aware of this and is deliberately distancing herself, so I'm not unduly worried about this aspect.

'Please write soon,
            Nancy
'P.S. It's Serena's birthday next week. Perhaps you could send her a card. She has no other family but us.'

Adam screwed up the letter into a tight ball and added a rider to his mother's philosophy of life—'Write no evil'. But he had accurately read between the lines, as she had meant him to, and his first impulse was to anger, sharp and harshly critical.

Didn't the dedicated doctor, supposedly versed in human reactions, know that it was the patient who became infatuated with him—not the reverse? Adam realised in himself a primitive violence that wanted to beat senseless an anonymous figure an ocean away, and while it lasted, one unfinished threat drummed through his head— 'if he'd touched her'.

It remained after the fierce, blinding anger subsided, but served to deflect the disgust back at himself as it recalled one crazy minute out of time when he had wanted to do just that . . . to touch Serena, to more than look at her frail beauty. The memory was clearer than any collected since, more real to him than yesterday. And it never failed to leave a bitter taste in his mouth which no amount of whisky could wash away.

Now his mother expected his impartial judgement when a confusion of guilt and inexplicable anger tied his stomach into knots every time he thought of her little fledgling. Involuntarily his eyes strayed to the painting of Serena's mother. It didn't match the print of his memory, the expression too calm and trusting, but there was enough of the girl there to disturb.

Julia's mouth went into an even tighter line when she entered the study and found Adam staring at the portrait she instinctively disliked. She slammed the door and fired at his back, 'Where the hell have you been?'

Adam swivelled slowly round and the smell of some perfume, exotic and sensuous, filled his nostrils. He relaxed back in the desk chair and for the first time in months was conscious of her as a woman with more than a passing claim to beauty. But despite his appreciation of her bold features and generous curves under clinging blue silk, he knew with the utmost certainty that he would never again want her in his bed. He continued sipping his Bourbon in silence, but something in his look must have prompted the tirade that followed.

'I don't know why I agreed to come to America with you,' Julia cried plaintively with all the pathos of a tragic heroine, but when it failed to evoke a response she continued stridently, 'Adam Carmichael—the Great Lover, the Great Writer. What a joke! Ever since you came back from that trip to Yorkshire, the only affair you've been

capable of conducting is with that damn bottle. You're
nothing but a . . . an impotent drunk!'

The moment Adam lifted his head and turned his gaze
full on her, Julia stepped back, frightened she had
gone too far, but his reply was mild and amused. 'You
missed out the key to my fatal attraction—a *rich* impotent
drunk.'

He could have said more—reminded her that he had
never asked her to come to America. She had turned up
uninvited on his flight, and he had no delusions as to why.
Julia, having run through her divorce settlement, had
needed a meal ticket, and more than a little drunk when he
had reached his stopover in New York, he had allowed her
to earn it in a bedroom in the airport hotel.

'You're a bastard,' Julia finally managed, for she had
no real defence to the implied accusation, other than the
fact she had once found the man as attractive as his
money.

'Granted,' Adam smiled.

Frustrated, Julia searched for a new line of attack and
alighted on what even she normally recognised as a taboo
subject since the day Adam had caught her reading the
first psychiatric report with a lurid interest.

'I see you've had a letter from your mother.' Julia went
to pick it up, but Adam was quicker. Too quick. 'Ah, how
is the dear little thing—the mad cousin?'

'Leave it!' Adam rapped out, rising to his feet and her
bait.

'Why so touchy?' she challenged.

'I shall not discuss this with you,' he dismissed coldly,
making for the door.

'What's she like, Adam? I'm curious.' Julia, suffering
from the insult of months of his total indifference, became
quite reckless with a sense of her power to hurt. 'Is she
physically deformed as well? Is that why you're too
ashamed to talk about her?' It stopped him dead in his
tracks and she observed his hands clenching into tight

angry fists. 'Or is she simply a social embarrassment? You know—bedwetting and dribbling at the mouth . . .'

'You ignorant bitch!' It was a roar, the only warning of the fist sent flying as he turned.

At the last second Adam caught the action up sufficiently to unfurl his fingers, but the back of his hand still had the force to knock her back against the desk. He could easily have broken her jaw if he had been a fraction slower.

'Don't come near me!' Julia screamed in genuine terror as he took a pace forward to try to do something about the damage he had done. It wasn't the first time Julia's vicious tongue had resulted in her being hit by a lover, but never by the cool self-controlled Adam, and that blow had been no emotional play-acting. She began to edge nervously along the desk.

'I'm not going to hit you again,' he stated raggedly, backing slowly away from her, hands loose at his side. 'Just don't talk about her like that.'

'I won't,' Julia promised, giving him one long frightened stare before rushing to the door with the parting shot of, 'Perhaps you should be seeing a shrink too!'

Adam's laughter followed her out into the hallway, a loud crazy-sounding confirmation of her fears. He had read her perfectly—wrongly assuming Serena Templeton to be a blood relation, Julia now had doubts about his own sanity. Yet she was close. There was a craziness in him, not through heredity but by infection. Through the touch of the girl. And realising the absurdity of that idea, he laughed all the harder.

'It's from the States,' Nancy declared with pleasure after a brief examination of the labels adorning the flat wooden crate. 'From Adam, for your birthday.'

Her birthday had been and gone. Nancy had bought her a beautiful chestnut mare, a generous gift all the more precious because it was a testimony of Nancy's faith in her recovery. Simon Clarke had given her an illustrated book on Renaissance painters, and it had embarrassed her. She didn't want any more presents, at any rate not this one.

'Aren't you dying to see what's inside, dear?' Nancy enthused brightly.

In many ways Nancy treated her as a little girl; it didn't annoy, because it was motivated by affection. Serena forced herself to move towards it, to smile and look excited, while every inclination cried out against touching the box.

'I wonder what it is?' Serena stalled, as she tried to banish her silly fears connected with the sender. At first the subject of Adam Carmichael had been avoided by his mother, but it had not been natural. And now when his name slipped into conversations, Serena schooled her features and gave a convincing pretence of having no memory of the man.

'It's nailed down,' she mumbled, as though that fact would prevent it ever being opened.

Brocklehurst came with hammer and chisel, and after much grunting and muttering, levered up the top and as if he was still in the stables emptied all the straw on the living room carpet.

'Eeh, it's thee, Miss Serena,' he finally announced, placing the painting with an unusual care against the back of the leather sofa so they could all admire it.

'It's my mother!' Serena cried with pure wonder. How many years had it been since her father had explained that the painting had upset Andrea and therefore had been given away? For a moment there was only utter pleasure in the gift.

'Fancy Adam finding it!' Nancy exclaimed proudly. Her son had not only remembered but sent something so special. 'There's a card. "To my cousin, with best wishes." Isn't that nice?'

With well-practised self-control Serena stopped herself from protesting aloud, 'He's not my cousin'. For though

she had accepted Nancy as her aunt, had grown very fond
of the woman who was so different from Andrea Simmonds, she could not eradicate a certain bad memory.

Not wanting to hurt the older woman, she lamely
replied, 'It's very kind of him,' but the words held none of
that first surge of joy.

Later, in her new airy bedroom, she stared hard at her
mother's portrait and then into the mirror. The same
features and colouring had been duplicated in herself, but
the likeness was superficial. Painting it when her mother
had already entered the last stages of consumption, the
artist had captured all her inner beauty and peace.

Had her mother ever feared that creeping death? Raged
against the unfairness of it? Serena didn't think so. Her
father had taken her into the garden of the small villa in
Italy and warned her that her lovely mother was very ill.

'You must be wrong, Daddy,' she had declared with the
total certainty of an eight-year-old in whose experience ill
people didn't laugh and dying people were like the old
woman with the gnarled hands and the bent back who had
once lived next door.

When she had been confronted with the truth of it, she
had none of her mother's calm strength to draw on.
Indulged by the local villagers and cherished by her
parents, she had cried hysterically against the hitherto
unknown pain, until her father forced her to recount and
hold on to all the happy memories of her mother. It had
helped, and to a certain extent, later when her father had
left her too, but there had developed darker shades of the
spoilt little girl who had cried, 'Daddy, I hate the whole
world!' No, she had too much anger in her to ever
approach her mother's serenity, and although she could
be 'good' for those she liked, she also knew herself capable
of the opposite.

Along with the painting Adam had enclosed a short
note giving his support for her going to college, thus
overriding Simon's advice. She should have been grate-

ful—instead she retained the impression that he was a
threat to her, based on one vivid recollection of the
good-looking face in Nancy's photograph bending over
hers and wanting to hurt her in a way that even Andrea
could never have matched. It was a fear she had never
quite learned to rationalise, but she wanted very much to
put Adam Carmichael into his true perspective.

First she penned a short thank-you note to him, its style
not much improved on those she had sent in her childhood
to a great-aunt in Scotland who used to knit her mon-
strous woollen cardigans and which she had worn for
precisely the thirty seconds it had taken for her mother to
snap her picture and send to the old lady. A duty letter,
and it read like it, but she would have been genuinely
amazed by the anger it engendered in its recipient.

Over the next few weeks, she read his books and used
her sharp intelligence to gauge the writer from what he
had written. She conceived a clear picture of a clever man
with a liberal twist of wry humour which made her smile
in spite of herself, and a cold, dispassionate view of his
fellow man, from which she quite wrongly deduced that
Adam Carmichael had more than a passing fondness for
himself. Added to the speculative kitchen gossip that she
had overheard concerning his private life, she had him
pigeonholed as an egotistical womaniser. Not a pleasant
image, but not a very frightening one either.

The day came for enrolment and Nancy drove her down to
the station, with both of them playing down the event. It
was early October and cold. Serena was wearing a blue
duffle jacket over jeans and a fluffy white jersey. She had
bought them and their like on a shopping expedition with
Nancy, who had favoured only smart, tailored clothes but
had accepted with good grace Serena's taste, based on
information she had culled from magazines.

Serena breathed a sigh of relief to find that her casual
clothes conformed with the norm, but it was the single

comfort she derived from the milling students gathered outside the college gymnasium. Not only did she appear to be the only person who knew no one else, but the conversations that drifted in her direction about films and modern music could have been in a foreign language for all she understood. She was struck by an echo—of being five years old and surrounded by dark Italian children chattering too fast for her modest command of the language—but even then she hadn't felt so bad, because she had hidden her shyness in her mother's skirts.

By the time the doors opened and the mass began to surge forward with some semblance of organised chaos, Serena was in full retreat, hugging the low perimeter wall. The yard emptied and she was left with the conviction that if she didn't make it today, she would never get this far again. It took her to the glass entrance but no further; the foyer was now deserted, and she had made it worse for herself by hanging back. Shrinking into the corner of the arched doorway, Serena felt ashamed of her cowardice.

'Are you going in or just contemplating the architecture?' a breezy teenage voice interrupted her apparent abstraction with the building's exterior. 'Late twentieth century functional, I believe.'

Serena's stare moved from the glass to the newcomer, but she remained aloof and the youth shrugged when his attempt at humour didn't raise an answering smile.

'Damn and blast!' The curse was directed at the stiff door that opened outwards and was proving difficult for the boy leaning heavily on a stick. 'Could you?'

And Serena, breaking out of her self-absorption, noticed for the first time that her companion was handicapped, and her own fear became secondary as she went ahead and opened the series of doors. That was until they reached the hall where the other students were casually scattered around, waiting for their names to be called, and then it came back to her full force when heads turned at the opening of the door and they were subjected to more than a cursory glance.

'It's OK. People always do that,' the boy announced when he caught and misread Serena's startled expression. 'Watch this.'

Serena did as she was told, while her companion glared fiercely at the nearest starer, whose face turned scarlet, and then muttered disgustedly, 'Like you had two heads instead of a slightly bent leg!'

The leg was more than slightly bent and covered by a heavy caliper, but Serena picked up from the tone a very clear message—'Pity me and I'll make you sorry for daring to!'

Remarkably the boy's abrupt manner made her lose enough of her diffidence to ask, 'I wonder if you could help me. I'm not sure what we're supposed to do.'

The boy held his head at an angle, testing Serena, discerned only a painful shyness and grinned the first overture of a friendship that was to enable her to survive the difficult weeks ahead.

They were an odd pair: Charlie, most extrovert and cheerful, sometimes cutting and abrasive, came from a Liverpool slum—the words he himself used—and stubbornly refused to paint anything he did not see as beautiful; while Serena, with her pretty manners and natural refinement, initially could only paint in her self-taught style, its almost savage intensity a complete mystery to her tutor and fellow students when contrasted with her quiet beauty. Yet they were friends.

Serena travelled the eight-mile round trip daily. She could have shared a flat with some of the other girls, but although with Charlie's help she was learning to bridge the gap created by her lost adolescent years, she did not feel part of her generation. It was a strange mixture of being too naïve and ignorant to understand their morals and trends, too adult and restrained to join in with their youthful high spirits. By evening she was glad to be at home with Nancy's less demanding company.

In the main she was content with the way life was—painting, riding and restful weekends—and it was through no effort of her own that she caught the attention of a local gentleman farmer in the Rippondale valley.

One brisk November morning she went exploring farther afield than usual and took a spill when Gypsy, the chestnut, decided at the last minute that she didn't like the look of a hedge directly in their path. Serena landed on the other side without any serious injury, but Gypsy's turn had been too dramatic and resulted in a pulled muscle. Luckily they were on relatively low farmland, but after an hour of leading the horse by her rein, Serena admitted she was conclusively lost. And Gypsy, who at a trot or gallop unfailingly knew her way home no matter how new the territory, was completely directionless at a limp. They skirted yet another field of cattle, but when the bolt on the gate defeated her and put the road on the other side out of reach, Serena subsided on to the stile, and horse and human looked disconsolately at each other.

Four fields back they had also drawn the notice of the farmer, standing on higher ground and surveying his land through a pair of binoculars, but when John Saxon finally caught up with them in his Range Rover, the word trespassing instantly fled his mind at the first sight of Serena rising to her feet on the other side of the gate.

'Am I on your land?' Serena asked ruefully. 'I've got a bit lost and my horse has hurt her leg.'

Banal words, but the voice, soft and shy, matched her angelic looks and completed John Saxon's fall. At that instant the girl could have driven a tank through his prize herd of cows and he would have smiled benevolently on!

For her part no ground shifted under Serena's tired feet. The young, blond farmer looked dependable, and with concern for her horse uppermost, she accepted his offer to stable her horse at his farm and call the vet from there, for she was seven miles from home and had been travelling in the wrong direction for the last three.

He brought Gypsy back the next day in a horsebox, and stayed to lunch. While he made sheep's eyes at an oblivious Serena, the older woman weighed up and heartily approved what she saw—a good-looking, solid young man in his twenties. It was a conspiracy without Serena's inclusion, and by the time John had been to dinner twice in the following week and she realised the nature of his interest, no subtle passivity could deflect it. It wasn't that John Saxon was arrogant or sure of his own attraction; he just didn't pick up the 'thanks, but no, thanks' signals which Serena was sending. He was to be forgiven that, Serena decided, for he was getting quite blatant encouragement from Nancy. And in the end it was to please Nancy that she went riding with him and from there progressed to more formal dates.

John was easy and uncomplicated and Serena liked him for it, but the strongest part of his attraction lay in the fact that he regarded her as the same. He had left unchallenged her vague explanation of childhood illnesses which prevented her from socialising much in the district, and unquestioningly accepted the quiet, pleasant girl she presented to him.

Unconsciously she used him as a yardstick of her normality, and within three months of their meeting, and after introductions to his large circle of friends, the personality she had adopted was second nature, and anything less wholesome was expressed through her painting.

But while John Saxon very quickly came to look for some token of commitment, Serena was content to drift slowly. They graduated from casual embraces to kissing, but she had found that a disappointing experience. His mouth moving on hers was nice enough, but the earth didn't move and the stars were light years away when she shut her eyes.

Very much still a student of life, Serena returned to her

ideas on sex—Adam Carmichael's novels. The love scenes, well written and convincing, had given her some conception of passion and primitive emotions, but re-reading them, Serena concluded that either fiction was more exciting or there was something wrong with her own reactions, for John, tall, blond and very good-looking, was surely a perfect model for the romantic hero. The latter was unpalatable. With a dismissive, 'Fraud!' she replaced the book on the library shelf, and from then on conditioned herself to expect less of her physical response to John. Conversely, it moved their relationship forward.

Christmas and New Year were over. Adam, who was just beginning to surface from a blur of nightclubs, parties and heavy drinking, was in the kitchen to fetch his regular breakfast.

'*Gracias*, Juanita,' he said, accepting the Mexican cook's liquid remedy for a hangover and her motherly disapproving clucking with a smile. Then going to the study, he made the foul-tasting concoction tolerable with a shot of Bourbon.

The study had become a genuine sanctuary, for Julia hadn't entered it since the night he had hit her. He still felt bad about it, even if the end result was good. He relaxed back on the swivel chair, shut his eyes and waited until the tomato and prairie oyster had effected their temporary cure.

The desk was a litter area of notes, unfinished manu-script and weeks-old mail. The notes went straight into the bin where they belonged and after a cursory glance the manuscript followed; it was supposed to be finished by the beginning of February, just a week away, but Adam didn't believe the studio expected it. He went through the bills and got cramp from writing cheques for Julia's extrava-gances. They had increased lately, and he suspected he was being made to pay for his physical assault. So be it. Even at her rate of spending, she would take years to get through his capital, and he doubted she would be around that long. Julia liked money, but she also needed male attention and admiration.

Eventually the pile dwindled until the square flat parcel was once more exposed to the light of day. Buried for weeks under a growing mountain of paper, yet he hadn't forgotten it. It had arrived with his mother's present of gold cufflinks and an accompanying letter, liberally punctuated with Serenas. He knew what it contained—the girl's duty offering. He recalled his mother's explanation.

'The dear girl is so modest she had to be pressed into sending two of her sketches. Much more interesting than my present for the man who has everything! I think the poor child's nervous because she knows from the paintings you sent up from London that you take a great interest in art yourself, but I'm sure you'll like them.'

Sometimes Adam found his mother's rosy outlook on life to be downright exasperating. Her dear girl's reluctance didn't stem from modesty or nervousness. Serena Templeton had hated him on sight, for reasons best known to herself, but neither of their brief encounters had given her cause to revise her opinion.

The childish scrawl on the label didn't promise much for the standard of the contents. He would have liked to throw it in the bin, but couldn't. He suspected both he and the girl were in the same predicament—natural inclination versus the desire not to hurt his mother's tender feelings.

How right he had been, was Adam's first thought after he carefully unwrapped the parcel, the paper inside protected by stiff cardboard backing. Every laugh line and age wrinkle was there, the soft, indulgent eyes and the half-smile that always shaped Nancy Carmichael's mouth. Drawn with love, and capturing his mother's grace and goodness with just pencil lead and blank paper. And how wrong, in another respect, for the girl was an artist.

The good feeling created by his mother's portrait caught Adam unprepared for the second sketch.

His first reaction—jolted out of him—was that it had to be by a different artist. Not the dear girl of his mother's letters but a kicking, biting Serena.

Ostensibly it was the meet of a foxhunt, done in water-colours. He had seen hundreds of paintings of similar settings with the usual hounds, horses and riders against a background of farm buildings—but the similarity was superficial. This was no glorification of the hunt, for every face was transformed with an ugly snarl of teeth, wildly disproportionate to the other features. Her people were baying for the blood of the fox—a clever satire that disturbed as it was meant to. But it was more than that—it was a passionate explosion of bad feeling towards the sportsmen and women.

Adam placed the two pictures next to each other. How in God's name did his mother not see that her shy, pleasant girl was only one half of a true image, that her bright child was hiding a much darker soul? But then his mother had a tendency to accept people at face value—if the painting didn't fit her conception of the artist, then she obviously didn't understand the art, for the girl was everything she could have wished her to be, fulfilling the early promises of the lively child she had first met. Discount the intervening years.

So what could he do, six thousand miles away? Dear Mother, I am picking up some powerfully bad vibrations from your protégée's handiwork. Dear Mother, your little princess is an illusion created for your benefit by one hell of a clever artist. Either would be very effective in alarming her, but he doubted if the alarm would be directed at Serena. He had his answer—he could do nothing.

He emerged from the study to find an uproar of profess-ional caterers, preparing for one of Julia's increasingly popular parties, and he escaped to make one of his rare appearances at the film studio. He kept up the connection to give his life some semblance of direction.

The day went from bad to worse. By pure coincidence he found himself present for the pre-release showing of the film of the last script he had turned in months ago. Halfway through the screening he got up and left, making for the nearest bar.

He drank his first Bourbon in one swallow, and ordered a refill. Sensing someone at his side who was ready to strike up a conversation, he stared straight in front of him. By now he was used to the American habit of talking to total strangers in public bars; America was full of lonely people.

'You're Adam Carmichael, aren't you?'

Normally he might have responded; but now he took up his drink and moved to a booth in the back of the darkened drinking hall. The stranger followed him, and Adam wondered at the man's persistence in the face of his pointed rudeness.

'Should I know you?' Adam demanded tersely.

'We have met.'

Adam gave the thin intelligent face a short appraisal before saying, 'I don't remember.'

'You wouldn't.' The man smiled. 'You were quietly, reservedly but decidedly drunk at the time.'

'I'll take your word for it, Mr . . . ?'

'Stacy, Peter Stacy.'

'Weren't you . . . ?' Adam stopped himself from being brutally tactless.

'Yes, I used to be Peter Stacy, the writer—about a hundred years ago.'

'You had talent,' Adam remarked offhandedly.

'Always nice to meet a favourable critic,' the American laughed self-mockingly.

'Look, Mr Stacy, I don't mean to be rude, but why are you so interested in talking to me?' Adam wanted to be alone. 'I assume you're not starting a society for has-been authors.'

The American did not seem perturbed by the dry sarcasm, as he signalled a waiter for a repeat of his order, before replying musingly, 'Is that how you see yourself?'

'Skip it!'

'Actually I was at the preview,' Peter Stacy pursued. 'Bad, wasn't it?'

'Chronic was the word I would have used,' Adam muttered sourly. The stranger was nothing, if not honest, but Adam didn't want to go into any deep analysis of the film.

'I was watching your face, Carmichael,' Peter Stacy continued, reverting to seriousness, 'and I thought it only fair to tell you that you didn't write that screenplay.'

'I admit I didn't stay for the credits, but I seem to vaguely recognise the plot.' Adam's sardonicism was heavy, but seemed only to encourage his fellow drinker's need to talk.

'Vague would be the operative word. I suspect you were bombed out of your mind for three-quarters of the time,' the American writer commented wryly, and ignoring Adam's steady gaze that clearly told him to mind his own business, went on to explain, 'I read the original script.'

'You have my sympathy.'

'Don't be too hard on yourself, Carmichael,' Peter Stacy countered, picking up on the self-disgust in Adam's tone. 'In places it touched some quite enviable literary heights before wandering off into total obscurity.'

'What I saw seemed perfectly straightforward,' Adam took another swallow of his drink, and added bitterly, 'Run-of-the-mill, basic, trite garbage.'

'The revised version, as per the Hamlisch tradition of commercialism for commercialism's sake,' Peter Stacy returned with his own brand of cynicism.

At last Adam realised the man's involvement. He was a script consultant, or less politely put, a hack. Adam recalled his brutal assessment of the film and tried to backtrack, but Peter Stacy cut in with, 'Don't insult me. I used to be a writer too, remember. And you did a pretty similar job on your second script, although I suspect you were amusing yourself at the time.'

'Why do you do it?' Adam's interest was aroused; on another day he might have liked the man.

'Not for laughs, anyway. About the time I stopped finding anything I wanted to write about, I developed a hobby similar to your own.' Peter Stacy's bloodshot eyes rested momentarily on his neat gin. 'Sound like a familiar road?'

'Maybe.'

'You British are damned reserved.' There was no insult in the remark.

'Is there some point to this discussion, or have we passed it?' Adam felt the man was holding a mirror up in front of him, and he didn't like the reflection he saw.

'Perhaps you're made of sterner stuff than me, Mr Carmichael. I sincerely hope so.' The older man, having said his piece, got to his feet, and said with a wry smile, 'But I suggest you give any more previews a miss.'

'I may just take your advice, Mr Stacy.'

Despite the tone of the conversation, the parting hand-shake was firm. Adam understood the man's motive and there was a thread of decency in it, absent from the rest of his experience of Hollywood, where people used and abused each other with seldom a second thought. Perhaps he had done his own fair share of abuse, even if most of it had been directed at himself.

He ordered another Bourbon after Peter Stacy had departed, left it unfinished and headed for the coast road. Corny but true, the sound and sight of an ocean washing on to a deserted beach did have a cleansing effect. A cold January wind whipped through his clothes and cleared his head. He walked a few miles of sand, an incongruous figure in a smart lounge suit, stained and then soaked by the spray of the incoming tide. He stayed for the sunset over the Pacific, the only memorable spectacle in the year and a half of his life he had just wasted.

When he finally took himself home, the house was crowded and noisy with Julia's party. Stopping halfway up the stairs, Adam turned to view the scene with the detached eye of a man looking at another species conducting a meaningless ritual. In one corner he could see Julia fully engrossed with Melvin Hamlisch, confirming his suspicion that she had set her sights on a more secure lover than a drunk with a rapidly diminishing interest in just about everything.

He wished her well—he had been no prize—and said aloud and to himself, 'I think it's about time I went home.' The thought had been there since the morning, but he wasn't ready to admit what had put it there.

CHAPTER FIVE

'ADAM! It's so marvellous to hear your voice!' Nancy's delight was genuine and warming.

'And you too, Mother. How are you?'

'As fit as an old woman like myself has a right to be,' she replied with a tinkling laugh. 'And you and Julia?'

'I'm fine, Mother,' he replied, avoiding the enquiry over Julia. Despite retaining the morals of a different era, his mother had adjusted and come to accept that her son was living with a woman with no intention of marriage.

'I was getting worried . . . it's been a while . . .' she trailed off, knowing of old that Adam disliked her worrying about him.

It was therefore surprising when he said, 'I'm sorry I haven't written lately, but you know how it is.'

She didn't know how it was, for the few short notes he had written had been devoid of anything remotely resembling the truth, but believing him engrossed in the film world, she replied pleasantly, 'Yes, I understand, dear, how busy you must be. I'm glad you telephoned—I have some exciting news that I'm bursting to tell someone! I've been sworn to secrecy, but as you're six thousand miles away . . .'

Adam used this opening and his mother's pause for breath to say, 'Actually, I'm not.'

'Not what, dear?'

'Six thousand miles away. I'm in London.' He delivered this information clumsily. 'Mother, you haven't fainted on me?'

'Adam, what's wrong?' Nancy's voice rose with nervous alarm. 'You sound strange.'

'Nothing's the matter, mother,' he replied firmly. 'I've just returned to England, that's all. America palled.'

'I thought Julia loved it.' Nancy Carmichael was struggling to take in the fact her son was home; his occasional letters had not suggested any discontent—quite the opposite.

'She did . . . does,' he amended. In the end the parting had not been bitter. Adam had been polite and allowed Julia to pretend that she was leaving him for her rich producer who believed 'English' and 'class' were synonymous and was going to make her wife number four. Reluctant to fill the pregnant silence with drawn-out explanations over the telephone, he continued, 'I'll tell you all about it when I see you. Now what's this exciting news of yours?'

'It'll keep,' Nancy murmured distractedly, then pressed, 'When should we expect you, Adam?'

It was Adam's turn to fade off the line while he summoned up an impersonality for his enquiry of, 'What about the girl?' After all this time he should have been indifferent; he wasn't.

'Serena—she'll be delighted to meet you at last. I've told her all about you,' Nancy replied brightly.

'We have met before, Mother,' Adam pointed out dryly.

'Oh, she's forgotten that . . . that unfortunate misunderstanding,' Nancy airily dismissed his unspoken concern. 'Now when should we kill the fatted calf?'

'Tomorrow?' Adam suggested, slightly bemused by his mother's ability to gloss over any unpleasantness.

'Splendid!' she exclaimed unreservedly. 'I'll meet you at the station.'

'That won't be necessary, Mother. I've bought a car.'

'That was quick! How long have you been in London?'

'A couple of weeks.'

He heard the faint murmur of disappointment that he hadn't bothered to make contact on arrival, but he could not explain even to himself his fear of returning north—a fear that warred with a need to see for himself the evidence of Serena Templeton's remarkable recovery.

'Will Julia be coming up with you?' Nancy enquired tentatively.

'No, Mother, she's still in the States,' Adam smiled as he imagined his mother's relief at this news, although she was too polite to express it aloud. Before she could press for more information he added, 'Look, I'll satisfy all your maternal curiosity when I get up there.'

'I doubt it,' she laughed, knowing how reserved Adam could be about certain parts of his life, 'but I'll enjoy trying to prise the details of the last eighteen months out of you!'

'I'll look forward to the third degree,' he joked in the same vein, before ringing off.

He stopped halfway up the long sloping driveway and stared up at the house. It looked less grim than he recalled—a fresh coat of paint to the window frames, perhaps, and certainly a more colourful display of flowers in the surrounding flowerbeds for his mother was a keen gardener. He felt nervous—and at the same time annoyed that he should be so. For several seconds his hand hovered between first and reverse gear.

His mother must have been waiting at a window, for she came out on the forecourt just as he was pulling up in the year-old Porsche he had found in a West End garage.

She looked him over before exclaiming brokenly, 'Oh, it's good to have you back, son!'

'Tears, Mother!' he chided gently, but was himself touched by the warmth of her greeting. They walked arm in arm into the house, and most of the initial awkwardness had disappeared by the time they sat down to afternoon tea.

Adam lounged back on a deeply-padded armchair and surveyed the rest of the room. The antique writing table and Chinese lacquered display cabinet he recognised as favourite pieces from their London home, but the brown and cream patterned carpet and toning velvet curtains were new and the leather suite, rosewood occasional tables and sideboard were recently acquired antiques.

'You've done wonders with this room,' Adam complimented her transformation of a dreary lounge into a gracious but comfortable room.

'We've done the whole house,' Nancy glowed with some of the pleasure that had entailed. 'We had great fun at house auctions when we finally screwed up enough courage to bid.'

They conversed on the same lines throughout tea, until Adam caught himself counting the number of times his mother prefixed her sentences with the pronoun 'we'. He still couldn't put the question that had been in his mind since he stepped out of his car and automatically lifted his eyes to the end window. Where is she? A natural enough question, but somehow he didn't think he could make it come out sounding as such.

In the end Nancy pre-empted him with, 'Serena's so looking forward to seeing you. As it's the weekend she's out riding, but she should be home soon.'

'Are you sure?' Adam quizzed his mother's first remark and received a perplexed frown. 'That she's looking forward to my visit?'

'Yes, of course, Adam,' she assured him after the barest of pauses. 'She wants to meet her generous cousin who sends her such lovely presents from America.'

Said with complete blandness and a light, teasing laugh it made any reply Adam might have made utterly impossible. 'The girl is not my cousin, nor do I want her to be. The girl once believed I was going to rape her. And I doubt that she possesses a memory as conveniently short as you imagine!'

'You won't believe the change in her,' Nancy ran on with enthusiasm and maternal pride. 'It's marvellous!

Wait till you see . . .' She broke off on catching the shutting of the front door and rose spryly to her feet, saying, 'That'll be her now, I think.'

The eagerness in Nancy Carmichael's tone and step was unmistakable, but it was not shared by her son, who stayed rooted to his seat, not joining his mother, who went out in the hallway to greet the girl. Yet he found himself listening—straining to catch the sound of Serena Templeton's voice, wondering if it would match his memory of it, and in that moment he wished he had fought harder against the spur that had taken him back to this house.

He rose automatically as she entered, ushered in by a smiling, confident Nancy like a treasured prize. The impact the girl's appearance had on him could not have been predicted, and as they met head on, his defences crumbled. Dressed in immaculate riding outfit of fitted check jacket and cream jodphurs, her shapely legs encased in knee-high leather boots, she had her hair caught in a bun which the wind had slightly disarranged, leaving wisps of fine fair hair to soften the effect. She had an aura of vitality and grace—and her face, still fine-boned, but no longer with an unhealthy pallor, had grown into an almost exact replica of her mother's.

'How nice to meet you, Mr Carmichael,' she said politely as she came forward to take the hand he was extending.

His stomach muscles tensed painfully at the first touch of her small cold hand, and he forgot to shake it. Just held it in his, unconsciously moving his thumb over her slender fingers, until she raised her head. Her cheeks flushed delightfully as she realised his appraisal, but nevertheless she returned it with a steady measured look of her own. And for once Adam was incapable of shielding his own emotion—he felt his eyes must be telling her exactly what he was thinking—that she was the loveliest living thing he had ever seen.

'You must call me Adam,' he said, barely above a

murmur, and then instantly wished he hadn't spoken at all. He could have held her longer with silence, while she seemed to be doing her own accounting of him with her wide expressive eyes.

With her gaze sliding away and her hand wriggling out of his grasp, her tone increased in coolness.

'I'm sorry I couldn't be here to welcome you, but I'd already arranged to go riding with a friend. I'm glad to meet you at last, Nancy has told me so much about you.'

It was a pretty speech, delivered with a perfect composure that Adam strove to match, while his pulses still beat erratically.

'That sounds ominous,' he groaned amusedly. 'I hope she's left us some secrets to discover about each other in the coming weeks!'

Green eyes came flying back to his face, and recognising immediately that his choice of words had struck a wrong note, Adam tried to charm her wariness away with a smile that usually guaranteed a favourable response from the opposite sex, but judging by the mounting signs of her alarm, it proved wildly off target.

It was at this point that Nancy, watching the interchange with an increasing misgiving, interceded with an effort to keep her tone light and teasing, 'Serena, you'll have to be quick and go and change if you're going out tonight. Although John wouldn't object to anything you did, dear, I think an evening dress would be more appropriate.'

'Mm, yes.' Serena turned towards Nancy, and Adam alone registered the complete blanking off of the hostility which had faced him seconds before.

'Run along, dear, or you'll be late,' Nancy urged, successfully excluding Adam from any further conversation until she had whisked a willing Serena out of the room and then leaned wearily against the tightly closed door.

'Who's John?' Adam growled, his face a tight angry mask.

'I thought you'd got over it,' Nancy shook her head in despair, ignoring the question that seemed so revealing.

'I don't know what you're talking about, Mother,' Adam said harshly, and retreated to stare out the far window, while he schooled his features into a cold remoteness.

Nancy followed him there, pulling him round to face her with a surprising strength.

'This is one area where you will not intimidate me into silence, Adam!' Frustratedly she met his shuttered indifferent expression, but pursued the subject with a determined, uncustomary vigour. 'Perhaps you'll be more prepared to talk honestly when you've picked your heart off the floor.'

'You talk like a romantic novel,' he sneered.

'Maybe I do. And Serena is certainly the beautiful heroine, but there is no way, no way at all that you figure in the story. Not one with a happy ending, anyway.'

Adam visibly winced but muttered stiffly, 'I think you've made your point.'

He turned back to study the view from the front of the house, but his tightly clenched jaw told its own story and Nancy reverted to a quieter tone.

'Adam, I love you, but I love that girl too—almost as though she were my own.'

'So?'

'So you're too old for her,' Nancy supplied softly.

'Mother!' he snapped, 'you don't know what you're saying. I've only just met the girl.'

And still his eyes remained locked on the grounds beyond the house.

'I know Serena and I know you too, Adam. There's a vein of cynicism that runs right through your make-up which frightens me.'

'Do you want me to leave?' Adam demanded.

'No, Adam,' Nancy cried anguishedly, 'I want you to stay and chase away any last ghost that may remain with the girl.'

'Apparently she didn't even recognise me,' Adam stated coldly.

'It's difficult to tell,' she said innocently. 'She jealously guards her innermost feelings as though she feels people will use them against her. That you have in common.'

'And you trust me with your little princess?'

She frowned at the description. 'If you give me your word that you will be nothing more than polite and friendly,' she sighed, laying down her conditions. She had missed neither the look in his eyes when he first saw Serena nor the much-practised, lazy smile that had followed it.

'Why are you so sure I would harm her?' Adam asked.

'You wouldn't be able to help yourself,' Nancy murmured, faint but audible, and resting her hand on his sleeve, pressed gently, 'Have I got your promise?'

Adam looked down at his mother, caught the mute appeal in her soft blue eyes and backed his nod of acquiescence with a return to offhandedness. 'Don't worry, your little princess is quite safe with me. I'll grant I'm mildly attracted, but as you say, she is a little unsophisticated for my tastes.'

Swivelling round, he shoved his hands in his pockets and smiled sardonically. 'Perhaps the wilds of Yorkshire will provide another source of amusement.'

'In all other respects, you can go your own way as you always have.' Nancy was partially reassured by Adam's flippant attitude. Earlier he had brushed off his affair with Julia Montague with a careless shrug. Perhaps her overprotective attitude to Serena had, after all, made her exaggerate Adam's interest. 'I'd like you to stay as long as you want. This is your home, son.'

'Legally, maybe.' The crease of her forehead told him he was upsetting her. 'Well, Mother, I'll take you up on your offer and remain here until I get restless again.' This time his smile was warm and genuine.

Nancy Carmichael sighed relievedly. One thing she

had not foreseen was a favourable personality change in her son; it was hard to define, but it was definitely there. She matched his altered mood, giving her tinkling musical laugh.

'I can't see you settling for long, Adam. You've got too much vitality to bury yourself up here—to quote your own words.'

'Mm, time alone will tell,' he conceded as they returned to the warmth of the fire. 'However, I would certainly appreciate some peace and quiet to work on a new novel.'

'I haven't been able to get hold of your most recent book.' Although she did not grasp some of the ideas in his novels and was perturbed by others, she enjoyed them. Whether through maternal pride in his achievement or because of their literary content, it was difficult to judge. 'Was it only published in the States?'

'I haven't written a book in two years,' he explained evenly, shaking his head to his mother's offer of a drink. 'I was writing screenplays in Hollywood.' He fervently hoped the films had not preceded him to this country.

'Serena said it was probably that,' Nancy declared. 'She saw a film with your name on the credits. I was going to see it . . .'

'But?' Adam prompted with an element of humour.

'Well, Serena said it wasn't really suitable for anyone over twenty-five or under eighteen. Although I must confess I didn't understand what she meant by her remark, and by the time I decided to go and see it, it was no longer showing in Leeds.'

Adam knew exactly what Serena's criticism implied. 'You didn't miss much,' he denigrated the sensationalism he had injected in a mood of black humour. He hadn't seen that second film, but he could imagine. 'Not some of my better work, I'm afraid.'

'Oh, I don't think she meant that,' Nancy defended hastily, and because she was still optimistically hoping that a friendly relationship could develop between the two, she added truthfully, 'Serena's read all your books, you know—she's a great fan of yours.'

'Really?' Adam's disbelief was concealed behind the succinct reply. Any notion that Serena Templeton now saw him in a favourable light had been destroyed by that half-suspicious, half-defiant look she had bestowed on him before leaving the room. Suddenly he didn't want to talk about the girl any more. Bending down to brush his mother's pink powdered cheek with his lips, he excused himself. 'I think I'll go and unpack before dinner.'

For a long while Serena sat on the window seat, a motionless figure, hugging her trousered knees and staring out into the approaching twilight, her mind scattered in all directions as she tried to make sense of her reaction to him.

It wasn't as if she'd had no warning—a full twenty-four hours to practise the fixed smile and the right notes of polite welcome. She had been so sure of herself when she walked into the room. Perhaps that confidence had been her mistake.

His voice, so deep and sensual, had been the test. She had swallowed silently, quelling the excitement engendered by his touch, and trotted out the rehearsed greeting. Controlled and pleasant, it came out word-perfect. She was going to pass.

And then suddenly it had gone wrong. What was it he had said? She couldn't remember, not exactly. Something about secrets. Triggering off an overreaction, her head snapped up and she clashed with eyes that no longer looked soft and melting. Devouring eyes. Andrea's smile spreading over firm, well-cut lips. It had thrown her wildly off balance and wrenched her back to the dark time.

She was there now. Slipping—she had to keep moving—continue to run from those bad memories. She jerked her legs to the floor and brought herself firmly back to the present. She heard the crunch of gravel and looked down as Adam unloaded his suitcases.

Lithe, muscular . . . almost the perfect tall, dark and handsome, she thought, and yes, for a second, she could see him again as a physically superb example of his sex. It wouldn't be normal, she said to herself, if she hadn't been initially impressed by his arrogant brand of good looks—but take them away and what was left? A middle-aged writer, bankrupt of ideas, judging by the film she had seen, but rich enough to indulge a taste for the supposed good life which she did not need to experience first-hand to disdain. Just a man who made it a dubious point of honour to charm any member of her sex. Nothing sinister. Nothing she couldn't handle.

After half an hour of flurried activity, she descended the broad sweep of stairs with an uncharacteristic haste, not stopping to analyse her urgency to be waiting for John when he called. He was always punctual, to the minute, but normally he had a drink in the lounge when she, often as not, failed to live up to his excellent timekeeping.

In the hall mirror she squinted critically at her reflection. The dark green velvet suit and cream silk shirt looked right—cool and stylish—but the hair floating free past her shoulders was definitely not. Too wild by far. She checked her watch. Five minutes. She tipped her head forward and a cloud of silky straight hair obscured her vision as she prepared to clip it into a neat topknot.

'It's longer than I'd imagined.'

At the soft, low words, Serena forgot her errant hair as her head jerked up and she backed hard against the cause of her fright. Firm hands reached out to steady her while her fairness streamed back from her rapidly paling face in total disarray. And there in the highly-polished glass, her frantic eyes sought and held his dark fathomless stare. His sudden appearance had deprived Serena of nerve and she shied away from the hand that lifted from her shoulder as though it was about to strike her.

'Don't be frightened,' Adam murmured as he stroked the tumbled hair back with a disarming slowness.

He was smiling at her reflection, a lazy spreading of his sensual mouth that tightened the constriction in her dry throat. Surely she could handle this man!

'What do you want of me?' she challenged huskily at the mirror when he resisted her attempt to slip from his loose grip of her shoulder.

His eyes travelled slowly over her reflected features before ending at her pink trembling mouth. 'I'm not sure yet.'

But Serena, emerging from the mental corner into which she had fled, recognised the nature of his threat as accurately as if the long brown fingers resting on her jacket had made a blatantly sexual exploration. It burned her skin to a blushing red.

She didn't fully understand how her reaction only touched on fear before becoming something that mingled pain with pleasure, but she knew she had felt it once before—and caused by the same man. The same man she had fought coming out of the nightmare that had plagued her sleep. So vivid the memory that she almost screamed in a faithful reproduction of the scene, and bit hard on her lower lip to stop herself doing so. She met his penetrating gaze again in the mirror and read the hard, hurting doubts about her sanity as his eyes darkened to near-black. For a second the sight of the small spot of blood forming on her self-inflicted cut held them both. And then he moved away from her, out of her range as she turned to face him, her fingers unconsciously clenched at her side, refusing to stretch out for the handkerchief he was offering, and betray their trembling.

Thrusting the white linen back into the pocket of the black cords which moulded his long muscular legs, Adam looked directly at her and said with a strangled harshness, 'You remember me, don't you?'

'Yes.' One word, but it held a note of fierce defiance against what Serena imagined to be his anger. Maybe the notion that he had returned to destroy her fragile peace

wasn't pure fantasy. The girl who had come through years
of her stepmother's emotional battering trained expres-
sionless green eyes on her new adversary, and her very
stillness, like a lifeless doll, became a weapon in the silent
battle of wills that followed.

It lasted minutes and could have lasted hours if the
sound of gravel being thrown up in the front driveway had
not cut into the building tension that threatened to enclose
them in their own private world.

Adam was the first to find his voice, and with the echo of
the past filling his mind he gave a commitment, muted
with intense feeling, 'I am with you. Believe me, Serena,
this time I am with you.'

Serena understood neither the words nor the tone, but
concentrated on one thought. Adam Carmichael was her
enemy.

She didn't wait around to witness his startled reaction
as she broke free, and with her mind on flight rather than
direction, she slammed the front door behind her and
cannoned blindly into John Saxon's arms.

'Hey, what a welcome!' he muttered appreciatively as
he held her at arm's length. 'I must come late more often!'

'Late?' Serena repeated distractedly.

'Yes, ten minutes,' John smiled down at her. 'We'd
better rush. The table's booked for seven-thirty.'

He didn't have to hurry Serena into the car. She almost
threw herself into the passenger seat of the large sedate
Daimler that had belonged to John's late father. John
didn't notice her urgency, however, nor did he remark on
her monosyllabic replies as he drove them to the country
hotel which boasted the best cuisine in the neighbour-
hood. The young farmer was used to her spells of quiet-
ness, rather liked their undemanding nature.

But long after they were settled to their meal, less than
half of Serena's attention was centred on the plush,
old-fashioned dining room of the Rippondale Royal.

'Penny for them,' John Saxon teased as he realised his

monologue on Continental grain prices had fallen on deaf ears. Sometimes he wondered if he really knew the captivating girl who sat opposite him, toying with her food.

Serena started guiltily, raising her eyes from the tablecloth. Kind, uncomplicated John—she wondered how he would react if she gave voice to the chilling disturbance that was still rioting through her brain. My wicked stepmother—no, honestly, no fictional character from my once fevered imaginings—drove me to the edge of her madness and her nephew, the big bad wolf—yes, he really does have white teeth—has returned to help me make the last leap. Maybe it would sound absurd. It was absurd!

'Are you all right, darling?' John queried, frowning helplessly at the quicksilver emotions flitting across her face.

With a conscious effort, she arranged her mouth into a bright smile that effectively dispelled his anxiety. 'I'm sorry. Term exams, I'm afraid.'

'You'll pass,' John immediately responded to her hastily improvised excuse.

Serena caught his look of pure adoration and her guilt increased at her deception—not the little white lie she had just told, but the months she had allowed to pass without revealing any of her past, intent on living up to his image of her.

'Who was your visitor?' John gave way to curiosity, since Serena had failed to bring the subject up. 'The owner of the white Porsche?'

Serena's hesitation was fractional before she shrugged. 'Nobody important . . . a friend of Nancy's.' She wanted to belong to John's world, safe and predictable as the coming of the seasons. 'John, I was wondering if you still wanted me to come over to the house in the evening and help you clear up your backlog of accounts. Over the next month, say.'

'Your exams?' he reminded her in all fairness, although he was tempted to leap at her offer, because he was sure he would enjoy the loathed task if he had the right company.

'I'll pass, remember?' she laughed with a forced brightness, and at his evident pleasure, regretted using him this way. 'But if you'd rather not . . .'

'No, I'd love to have you over,' he broke into her objections, placing his hand on hers. 'It might help you decide. You know, being at the house. Us working together . . .' He trailed off, leaving the question he had asked weeks ago hanging in mid-air.

Serena, as usual when offered a place in his secure undemanding life, couldn't find the certainty which she knew she was supposed to feel. For the rest of the evening, however, she managed to keep her mind on his conversation, smiled at his boyish enthusiasm for his plans to improve the sizeable farm his father had left him. And when they parted in the porchway of Simmonds Hall, she allowed him a greater intimacy when his mouth eagerly covered hers, and again felt that sharp disquiet when his breathing told her he was becoming aroused while her brain still clicked away with a quiet cool precision. Unwilling to feign passion, she pulled gently away as his hand came nearer her breastbone.

'I have to go in,' she announced without anger.

John's disappointed but sincere, 'OK, I understand. I can wait,' followed her upstairs to her bedroom, and her unease grew as she stood in front of her mother's portrait.

'Never marry anyone you don't love,' her father had once warned her when they had climbed the hill behind the house. Up in their sanctuary he had been trying to explain the atmosphere back at the house which had touched her without giving her an understanding of the gathering storm which electrified it. But he hadn't been there when the lightning flashed, and without his loving protection, she had to do her own adapting.

She had survived, but she was now counting the cost, for she seemed to have lost the capacity to love anyone again. What she gave Nancy was a pale reflection of the love that flowed for the beautiful young woman who smiled at her. And the feeling she had for John never passed beyond a deep affection. So was it wrong to offer him the slightest encouragement, even if spending more time at his home provided her with a means of escape in the coming weeks?

Serena didn't know, but she had no choice if she wanted to avoid Adam Carmichael till he left—back to his mistress in America. Away from him, she could appreciate that any intentions lurking in his sleek black head were strictly directed at her body, not her mind. But she sensed a cool intelligence behind the façade of lazy charm that might be keen enough (if it chose to amuse itself at her expense) to detect and expose matters best left buried. Not that she was scared of him. She wasn't, she assured herself. It was just that she didn't want to upset Nancy who so obviously cherished hopes that theirs would be a friendly relationship.

Cousins!—it was laughable when her 'cousin' proceeded, the moment he got her on her own, to earn the reputation that his books and kitchen gossip had already established. His technique could not be faulted, nor its effects. For, even when she had been in John's arms, it was *his* lingering gaze that remained.

How many women had fallen for that old trick? Dozens probably, made suddenly, acutely aware of their own attraction. Stupid women who wanted to believe that they were special to the man who used his looks and studied charm as weapons.

And with this scathing dismissal of Adam Carmichael, she rose from the blanket box at the end of her bed, moved to the dressing table and brushed her hair till her scalp tingled from the vigorous strokes of the stiff bristles.

CHAPTER SIX

ADAM's days settled into a pattern, and the peace and quiet of the country proved very conducive to his writing. The novel, a satirical fiction on the movie capital of the world, went well; it was, to him, his best work in years. His mother gave over the study to him as it was at the far end of the house, and most afternoons, sometimes well into the night, he spent banging away at a typewriter with quick two-fingered efficiency. The sound was music to his ears after the literary stagnation in Hollywood.

Although his mother seemed to lead a very full social life, he made a point of dining at the table every evening. After his mother's warning on the first day and that brief, disastrous interchange with Serena, he had determined to be polite, to adopt a brotherly attitude to the girl and prove that he was no more affected by her than by any other of the beautiful women he had met in his life. But things did not work out the way he had planned. Instead his obsession with her grew, fed *not* by her continuous presence but rather by her elusiveness—for in the weeks he had passed in Yorkshire she had not once sat down to dinner with him.

His sole contact with the girl was the brief meetings in the corridor or on the stairs when she bestowed on him an automatic impersonal smile. On these occasions she appeared always to be rushing somewhere, but when he caught glimpses of her through the study window as she crossed the yard to the studio her pace was more leisurely. Dressed in formal evening wear, riding clothes or her casual college clothes, her fresh and flawless beauty never failed to have an effect on him, although he had learned to disguise the fact with an immobile, cold expression.

He should have been grateful that she had removed the burden of having to convince his mother that he had no evil intentions; in fact, Serena's contrived avoidance infuriated him. Strangely, this fury drove him to work even harder until the novel begun at the end of his days in California was finished in a few short weeks. Its completion, however, did nothing to quieten that taut, restless energy.

Within days he received word from his publisher, and although he said nothing to his mother save that he had to go down to London, he packed a large suitcase and took what he hoped was one last long look at the house before swinging in a wide arc and out of the gates.

He arrived late, stayed overnight in the Kensington house which had a neglected air after being shut up for two winters, and devoted the next day to the business that had ostensibly taken him away from Yorkshire.

After a preliminary discussion on money matters, he reached an easy agreement with his publisher and, the business settled, they went out to celebrate what Gary Hammond maintained, with his editor's sixth sense, was a sure-fire bestseller. Adam's enthusiasm was more restrained, but nevertheless he set out to get drunk over the lunch. Despite his abstinence in Yorkshire, several hours later he was still sober and rational enough to bundle a fuddled Gary Hammond into a taxi and wend his way back through a windswept Hyde Park. The walk was invigorating, but he didn't particularly want a clear head.

Stripping the dust-sheet off the drinks cabinet, he accidentally sent crashing to the floor one of his mother's innumerable photographs. He looked again at himself aged twenty and laughed at the absurd direction his thoughts took. He might have aged, but that diffident boy posing selfconsciously for the camera would not have possessed the remotest idea of the complex creature he sensed Serena Templeton to be. And yet with utter certainty he knew it would have been the same—the youth he had been would have been just as fascinated. Only he might have called it love. And what did one call it? Desire, yes, but more ... much more than that, he wanted to know all of her.

The next day he woke with a mild hangover and a strong compulsion to return to Yorkshire. It was insanity and he knew it, but being aware of it didn't stop him.

When he arrived, his mother had already left for her regular Saturday afternoon bridge game at the local club. He left his suitcase in the boot of his car and going straight to the lounge, unstoppered the whisky decanter. Again he found no solace in staring at the bottom of an empty glass, and the black cloud that had hung over his head as he shrugged off his suede jacket seemed only more ominous.

He went out by the bay window and found the ground hard under his feet. The spring day held a distinct chill as he skirted the glasshouse and headed for the white brick studio. Looking through the end window, he felt no relief that he had been able to find her; he knew he was about to behave very badly.

She was clothed in a surprisingly white smock, and tight blue jeans. Her hair was tied in a high ponytail, making him acutely aware of how young she was.

She didn't look up when he knocked, but her air of abstraction was not convincing, because he knew she must have either seen or heard him approaching the studio. He didn't speak but wandered round the room, picking up her canvases and examining her work—more out of a desire to annoy her into breaking the silence than out of genuine interest. Nevertheless he was struck by the rampant talent to which they testified. And they told him more clearly than words that the demure front she presented to the world was just that—a façade. They were mostly of people—not fixed lifeless portraits but real human beings revealing the whole range of their emotions.

'Did you miss me?' His question was sardonic and went unanswered. Serena's face in profile was a study of calmness and concentration as she continued to ignore him. 'No, I suppose not. Still, it must have been nice to be able to stay home for dinner.'

With a slight movement she presented her back to him and began to mix her paints. The gesture, rude and deliberate, snapped Adam's control. The palette snatched roughly from her grasp spilled its contents as he threw it angrily to the floor. He tensed for her response, the silence stretching his nerves. Slowly she bent to retrieve the wooden board, her eyes not having once moved in his direction. He pulled her upright and with a relentless grip on her chin, forced her head up.

'Damn you, say something!' he demanded harshly, and held on to her until she did.

She stared back at him, unblinkingly. 'I have nothing to say to you, Mr Carmichael.' Her voice was chilling.

'What happened to Adam?' Since the first day, she had addressed him by his first name during their infrequent short exchanges of pleasantries. 'Or are the little courtesies you occasionally bestow on me solely for my mother's benefit?'

'I have no wish to upset Nancy,' she acknowledged evenly, and reaching out for a cloth began to wipe away the paint that had spilled on her hands and arms. 'I assumed you wouldn't either.'

'So the house is designated as neutral territory,' he replied tightly when she confirmed his supposition without a trace of discomfort.

She slid him an oblique glance before retorting in her maddeningly cool, superior way, 'I didn't know we were at war.'

'Didn't you?' She was trying and, to a certain extent, succeeding in putting him at a disadvantage. He leaned back against the edge of the table and adopted a relaxed pose, before saying, 'You should, you know, because you initiated the hostilities from the very first day we met, and nothing's changed, has it?'

Her long lashes lowered fractionally, but she was all calm, slightly bored reason when she came back with, 'Really, Mr Carmichael, I don't know what you're talking about. One only fights over something one covets—or in self-defence. You have nothing I would ever want,' she declared disdainfully, and as though she could sense the further damage she could do, added a malicious, 'And I ceased being a frightened screaming child a long time ago.'

'I can see that,' he returned with an insolence as deliberate as her cruelty, his eyes resting meaningfully on her upper body where the cotton material stretched across her high breasts. Colour seeped into the slant of her cheekbones, and if anything, it made Adam feel worse.

'If you've come to insult me, Mr Carmichael, I suggest you do it now so I can get back to my work,' she muttered, half turning to her painting. The air was thick with her hostility towards him.

'The perfect little ice-maiden, our little princess has turned into!'

'Why do you call me that?' she swivelled round again.

'Little princess? Because that's what you are. A regal personage beloved by all her subjects—my mother, Mrs Baker . . .'

'But not by you,' Serena sliced into his explanation, picking up the harsh resentment behind it.

'Oh no, I'm a republican. Merely a guest at court,' Adam bantered back with the first trace of humour.

'Or the royal fool?'

'Perhaps,' he mused laughingly. It had been an attempt to put him in his place and she looked slightly disconcerted when it bounced off him. 'But remember, the jester, for all his apparent stupidity, often spoke the truth.'

'His or absolute?' Serena challenged bitingly.

She came back so quickly he wondered where he had

ever got the idea that she had to be treated with kid gloves.
He dropped his eyes from the glitter of hate that was in
hers, and positioned himself in front of her current painting that leaned on the easel. It was technically competent
but lacked the vibrancy of her other work.

'They have more than a smattering of brilliance.' He
gestured at her other efforts haphazardly strewn about the
studio. 'But this one's insipid—Maybe it's the model.'

His first comment tightened her mouth with disbelief, but the second had her sneering, 'From court jester
to art critic in two easy moves! Is there no end to your
talents?'

'Or yours?' he threw the accusation back at her. 'What
are your qualifications for the role of literary critic?'

She frowned darkly at him before admitting loftily, 'I'm
afraid, not having your quickness of intellect, Mr Carmichael, I can't follow that remark.'

'I wouldn't say that, Miss Templeton.' He was finding
her conversation, despite its asperity, a heady stimula-
tion, sharpening his own blunted wits. 'My mother informed me of your opinion on one of my screenplays. She
believes you're one of my biggest fans—but then she
didn't understand your criticism, being basically a sweet
soul.'

'But I'm sure you did.' Serena slanted him a look that
could have been read as impudence before she went on,
'Well, I'm sorry if you were offended.'

Behind the trite apology she was laughing at him,
despite her bland expression; the impulse to slap her hard
was killed by the memory of that other physical assault in
this girl's defence.

'You didn't offend me,' Adam growled, shoving his fists
deep into his pockets.

'It doesn't sound like it,' she mocked, and this time
there was definite evidence that she was enjoying getting
the better of him in the defiant sparkle of the eyes lifted to
his. 'Still, if it's any consolation, and I'm sure it will be, the

film made a lot of money, so some people must have found it . . . edifying.'

'Edifying,' he mimicked her derision. 'Do you think I measure the quality of my work by its commercial success?'

'Don't you?' she chipped back.

'No. And I don't need you to tell me it was unadulterated rubbish.' His brutal honesty held overtones of self-contempt and he felt momentarily exposed to her suddenly non-aggressive interest. His attention moved back to the painting. 'I still say your portrait is insipid.'

'You're entitled to your opinion, Mr Carmichael, even if no one asked you to give it.' Her reply lacked force, but Adam reckoned she was too clever not to know that the portrait did too.

'I haven't offended you, have I?' he murmured, shifting their positions.

'No,' she denied hotly.

'Oh, I am glad.' There was no ice encasing her now and Adam realised he was goading her into losing her temper. His eyes rested on her face as he asked, 'Who is he?'

'Who?' she snapped, deliberately obtuse.

Adam added, 'The adolescent Fauntleroy.'

'A friend,' she offered tersely.

'Well, he can't be a very close one, judging by your lack of . . .'

'It so happens, *Mr* Carmichael, that John and I *are* close, very close—not that it's any of your damn business!' she cut in, now near to shouting at him.

'Language!' Adam admonished irritatingly. He could see that she was hating him, but it was almost worthwhile because he was succeeding in reaching her. 'My mother hasn't the first idea of what makes you tick, does she?' He nodded at the painting. 'Does he, I wonder?'

'The game's over, Mr Carmichael.' Serena bent to pick up her palette and clattered it down on the table. 'Say what you have to say, then I can get on with my insipid painting while there's still enough natural light.'

'Game?' Despite the banter in which they had both indulged, Adam had taken it very seriously, and his innocence was not totally assumed.

'I'm sure there's a point to this little charade—or is it just an exercise to see how far you can push me before I crack. If it is,' she continued when he simply stared incredulously back at her, 'you'll need better weapons than I've seen today. I've already been through one reign of terror.'

Said without self-pity or drama, but the words seemed torn from her as she stood hating and defying him with her pain.

'My aunt,' Adam murmured rhetorically, her distress cutting into him like a whip. He had blundered too far and too fast. Softly he tried, 'What did she do to you, Serena?'

She realised the change in his tone but took it merely for a tactical ploy, laughing bitterly, 'You don't think I'd give you that sort of ammunition, do you?'

'Don't close me out, Serena!' he shouted, and startled by his own loudness, said very low, 'I want to . . .'

She cut him short. 'I repeat—why are you honouring me with your presence?'

'It could be that I want to get to know you better,' Adam suggested, struggling for an explanation which even he could understand. 'You are my ward, after all.' It sounded lame.

'No, it couldn't,' she retorted, 'and as for being your ward, that situation should be rectified in six months' time when . . .'

'I want to know why you're treating me as though I had some infectious disease,' Adam interrupted, the gentleness fast disappearing from his voice.

'I suppose you have to have it for your work—a vivid imagination, I mean,' she went on almost as though she hadn't heard him, 'but as far as I'm concerned, you don't even enter my landscape.'

'Completely indifferent, are we?'

'Yes,' she returned with a boldness that he had to admire because he suspected she knew quite well she was touching a nerve.

'Well then, you won't mind a little test, will you?' he said, stepping forward.

'If you lay a finger on me, I'll . . .' Serena swallowed back the rest of the reckless threat in flushing embarrassment when his hand failed to come near her but instead flipped a cover over John Saxon's portrait.

'You'll what—Scream rape? We've been through that scene before, remember?' Adam drawled. 'I've never had to force myself on a woman in my life, but if all that fiery defiance was an invitation to live up to my obviously bad reputation, I wouldn't like to disappoint you.'

'It bloody well wasn't!' she cried aloud as he drew nearer, a smile of pure mockery on his lips. 'My taste doesn't run to old broken-down rakes!'

Adam winced inwardly but made a semblance of recovery with, 'What a deliciously old-fashioned word! My mother thinks I might hurt you, Princess. I wonder why?'

There were frustration and speechless fury in the look she shot him before she presented him with her back. Adam moved round the side of the table and leaned casually against the wall, watching as she scrubbed her palette with a cloth dipped in turpentine. Strength and beauty defined her profile.

'Your test, Mr Carmichael?' she eventually asked in a tone that implied she was indulging a spoilt, irritating child.

'Oh yes,' he murmured, folding his arms across his chest. 'If you ask me to, I'll leave Yorkshire for good.'

Her head moved fractionally round, but if she was surprised by his offer, she hid it well. 'And what does that prove?'

'If you're completely indifferent to my presence,' Adam returned quietly, 'you won't lower yourself, Princess, to ask.'

It stilled her hands and she gave the matter her full concentration before coming back with a suspicious, rude, 'There's a flaw in your little scheme—how do I know you'll keep your word?'

'I've been keeping company with some very dubious people in the last few years,' Adam replied stiffly, her bad opinion grating on his nerves, 'but I think you can safely assume my word is still good for something.'

She didn't answer straight away, and when she did, her eyes never lifted from the table and her tone was condescending in the extreme. 'I wouldn't ask you for anything if my life depended on it!'

Inwardly he sighed, feeling as if he had just gained a reprive.

'Such indifference,' he mocked the anger that lay beneath the cool exterior. No child, this girl, but fire and ice—a thrilling combination that stirred the senses. 'I wonder what your loving would be like.'

'I guarantee you'll never find out,' she rallied back, the gleam in her eyes and the provocative set of her full mouth seeming to issue a challenge.

'I have patience,' Adam avowed softly.

For a moment his lazy smile put her out of her stride, but she managed to flash back, 'You'll need it—an inexhaustible amount!'

He caught her arm as she made her first move towards the door.

'One more thing.' He ignored the contemptuous glance at his hand gripping on to her upper arm, as he continued smoothly, 'If I really don't bother you, Princess, perhaps I may see you at dinner tonight. My table manners are impeccable, I promise. I keep my wolfish tendencies at bay, at mealtimes at least.'

Said lightly and with dry amusement, it almost startled

a laugh out of her, but she stifled the sound in her throat and for once the green eyes raising to his looked less than certain of every move.

'Why don't you try it?' Adam spoke his thoughts aloud.

'What?' she breathed back.

'A suspension of hostilities.' Unconsciously his hand moved up to her shoulder to mould the fragile bones beneath the cotton smock. And again he said what was in his mind, in the heart that had quickened as his fingers touched the rapid pulse at the base of her soft throat.

'If just once you looked at me without enmity, just once gave me a smile that was real, I could become one of your most loyal, most devoted subjects, Princess.'

Indeed the hostility left the wide expressive eyes, but no smile was forthcoming as she stammered her disbelief,

'I . . . I don't understand you?'

'Don't you?' It was suddenly clear enough to Adam. He had fallen in love, for the first time, with the girl backing slowly away from his caressing hand. 'I won't hurt you . . . not knowingly.'

It wasn't a taunt, Serena knew that, but suddenly she was scaring herself with her response to this man's soft undermining tone. She was poising for flight—Why did she hesitate?

'So will I see you at dinner?' Adam pursued.

'I don't know,' she said shakily before spinning round and breaking free of his influence.

Her ponytail swung wildly from side to side as she covered the open ground between the studio and the house. And only when she reached her bedroom and leaned weakly against the door did she regret her impulse to run. Unable to understand his feelings, she felt instead that she had exposed the sham of her indifference by her sudden flight.

It had all been going so well: in the last month with Adam's making no attempt to approach her again, she almost ceased believing in him as a threat. Their meetings had been rare; she saw to that. And even those had been manageable, because she kept on the move—always on the move.

Those first evenings were spent exclusively with John, but that was a mistake, because he had only taken it as a sign of a commitment which she was not ready to make. And the time that followed was filled with cinema dates, extra studying in the college library and those dreadful student parties where she felt so awkward.

With no hint of unease, Nancy seemed delighted that Serena was getting out more and enjoying herself, and pressed her to use the car as a reward for passing her test after Christmas. Still, even the growing sense of guilt for her deception was preferable to how she might feel if she subjected herself to more of Adam Carmichael's strange company.

She had only to hang on, keep avoiding him, until he returned to America.

As he showered before dinner, Adam whistled tunefully under his breath, an occasional satisfied smile flitting across his features; she'd be there, if only to glare daggers across the table—he was sure of it. He dressed with care in a black velvet suit and tie, and laughed at his reflection. It would take more than sartorial elegance to impress a princess!

He took the stairs two at a time and halted for a couple of seconds in the hallway to draw in a deep steadying breath. Entering the lounge for the customary aperitif, he registered his mother's surprise at his appearance as his sweep of the room ascertained she was alone.

'What's the occasion?' she teased as she rose to place a kiss on his freshly-shaven cheek, secretly pleased to see him looking so debonair. He had seemed a little strained since his return, although pleasant company after their slight disagreement in the beginning.

'I'm not sure yet,' he replied enigmatically.

'Sherry?'

'No, whisky. I'll get them.' he whistled as he poured out the drinks.

'Must have been a very successful trip to London,' Nancy commented on his evident good humour as he handed her the glass and relaxed back on the sofa beside her.

'London?' he repeated blankly.

'Where you've been for the last two days,' she reminded him frowningly; vagueness was certainly not one of her son's normal traits.

'Oh, yes. Fine. Great.' He exaggerated, trying to cover up for the fact that he had dismissed the time he had spent in the city completely.

'You sold your book!' she cried excitedly, believing she had accounted for his air of near celebration.

'Yes. Yes, I did,' he confirmed, but his attention had wandered from his London trip and his mother to the elegant gold watch on his wrist.

'You don't sound too bothered.'

Adam made no comment on her curious reply. 'Where's Serena?'

Nancy was taken aback by his totally unexpected if apparently casual query. It was the first time her son had challenged Serena's whereabouts, despite her usual absence from the evening meal. She had almost convinced herself that he had lost any interest in the girl.

'I don't know,' she murmured warily,' I think she's out with John.'

'She's in your care,' Adam's disappointment made him harshly critical. 'Surely you should know how and with whom she spends her time?'

'She's free, and almost over twenty-one,' Nancy delivered her smart quip with a lightness she was far from feeling, and was relieved to hear the dinner gong that forced them to abandon the conversation.

That relief was shortlived, for as they were taking their

seats at table, Serena suddenly appeared in the room wearing a white dress of broderie anglaise, waisted and full-length, simultaneously virginal and sexy.

Nancy Carmichael had never seen the girl look quite so stunningly beautiful, and it was obvious that Adam agreed with her as he stared quite openly at her. It did not take a supernatural power to realise that something had happened between her two children—as Nancy thought of them—and she was unsure, for the first time for whom she was most afraid, as she felt a shiver of apprehension run up her spine.

'I'm sorry I'm late,' Serena made her apologies in a breathless whisper, her glance barely touching Adam.

'Better late than never, Princess,' Adam muttered quite seriously, as he rose to his feet and came round the table to draw out the chair opposite his for the girl still hovering in the doorway. His smile was not returned as she held herself aloof, although permitting his courtesy of settling her down on the seat.

The first course served, Adam broke the embarrassing silence that developed. 'If I may say so, you're looking very lovely tonight, Princess.'

'Thank you.' Her stiff acknowledgement of the compliment was directed at the tablecloth.

It would not have been polite for Adam to ignore Serena's appearance, and yet something in his voice made Nancy Carmichael angry with her son.

'Don't call Serena that!' Nancy's sharp tone, if anything, heightened the tension, and she was then cross with herself for having said anything at all.

Adam was all infuriating innocence. 'What?'

'Princess,' said Nancy, quite unnecessarily, she was sure.

'Serena doesn't mind, do you?' Adam baited, and although she looked directly at him, she did not rise.

'No,' she affirmed coolly.

'After all, what more appropriate title,' Adam continued, his eyes encompassing the white bodice of the dress and the very pale skin exposed by its square neckline, 'unless it was . . . Snow White?'

'And does that make you one of the Seven Dwarfs?'

The girl's calm rejoinder caused an explosion of laughter from her son, but Nancy was far from tempted to a similar outburst. As disturbed as she was by his behaviour, it did not match the shock she felt at Serena's cool put-down. Never before had she seen that side of the girl's nature, the underlying toughness suggested by the remark.

'Which one?' Adam countered, when he regained control.

'I haven't decided yet,' Serena flipped back, with a sweet utterly false smile.

The older woman quickly stepped in, guiding the talk towards less personal lines by asking about his short trip to London. Had he seen any friends? Was the house in Kensington in need of external repairs? She chattered about how the capital was changing and how much she noticed this redevelopment now she no longer lived there. With a supreme effort she sustained this topic through most of the meal, but she was all too aware that Adam was allowing her to do this. Serena said little, but concentrated on her food, and when she was called to the telephone in between the main and sweet course, she quietly excused herself.

His mother launched her attack the second they were alone.

'I demand to know what's going on?'

'What makes you think there is anything going on?' Adam said, lifting an enquiring eyebrow.

'Drop the act of innocence—it doesn't impress me. In the rare moments you move your eyes off Serena's face, she starts watching you.' Nancy's mood was not improved by Adam's smile of satisfaction. 'What's happened between you and her?'

'Nothing,' he dismissed, but his mother added the qualifying 'yet' for herself.

'Adam, if you think . . .' Her angry words were bitten back on Serena's return.

He was glad of the halt to his mother's cross-questioning, even if it was based on the false assumption that Serena was too delicate for strong words. His interest shifted back to her face, and disregarding Nancy's disapproval coming from the head of the table, he noticed that her cheeks were flushed. He wondered what had caused the colour that on most women would have detracted rather than intensified her attraction for him. But then she wasn't most women. She was *the* woman, and the fact that he hadn't been waiting for her his whole life had made the discovery that much more difficult to accept.

The meal over, they returned to the lounge.

'Who was that on the telephone?' Nancy asked innocently.

'Only John,' Serena replied hesitantly.

'Is he coming over?' Nancy asked hopefully, for she liked John Saxon very much.

'No, he just telephoned because he half expected me over for dinner,' Serena replied in a quiet undertone that was solely for Nancy's benefit. 'Must have got our days mixed up.'

'Who's John?' Adam abruptly cut in, denying his apparent absorption in his cigar and brandy—and was surprised when Serena answered quickly,

'Just a friend.' Her direct look defied him to probe.

'He's more than that,' Nancy protested, unwittingly undermining Serena's attempt to kill the subject. 'Serena's too shy to tell you, Adam. John's the good news I hinted at weeks ago. I was going to leave Serena to tell you in her own good time, but . . .'

'Nancy!' Serena pleaded.

'Well, as Serena is too shy to tell me,' Adam drawled

with assumed nonchalance, 'perhaps you'd better, Mother.'

'He's a local boy with a very good background. Serena and he met while she was out riding one day in early November, and—well, it was almost love at first sight,' Nancy said happily, and stretching out to pour more coffee, missed the two pairs of eyes that met and locked, as she ran on, 'Anyway, just before your return he asked Serena to marry him, after having the good manners to ask me, of course.'

'Have you accepted?' Adam ground out, his dark thunderous stare willing her to deny it.

Serena's 'Not yet' and his mother's 'It's only a matter of time' were simultaneous.

'Stay out of this, Mother,' Adam instructed briskly. 'Which is it, Serena?'

'*It* has nothing whatsoever to do with you!' Serena shot back in the same tone as she had told him to mind his own damn business earlier in the day, before lowering her eyes dismissively.

He rose from the armchair where he had been lounging with a deceptive casualness and crossing the space that separated them, went down on his haunches directly in front of her. Ignoring his mother's startled exclamation, he gripped Serena's chin and forced her to look at him.

'Oh, but it has, Princess—make no mistake. As my ward you can't marry without my consent until you're twenty-one.' Time suspended, he felt her eyes duelling with his and respected the way she stared unflinchingly back at him.

His mother interrupted the silent contest of wills with an incredulous, 'Adam, you can't be serious! That's old-fashioned nonsense!'

Reluctantly he released the girl and straightened to face Nancy Carmichael, his normal detachment slotting back in place as he announced unequivocally, 'Oh, but I am—deadly serious.' The clause was specifically inserted in the will. And then as though the matter was sealed, he strolled back to his chair.

For a moment his mother was speechless. Her gaze flickered from Adam to alight on Serena, motionless and silent. Nevertheless Nancy was not content to leave it there.

'You have no right to interfere with Serena's plans!'

'Are you sure they're hers, and not yours, Mother dear?' he queried meaningfully.

Nancy was visibly distressed by his pointed accusation. It was true she was very keen on the match, had perhaps encouraged it, but only because John and Serena seemed so right for each other.

'John's a very nice boy,' she stressed defensively.

'Nice—mm,' Adam repeated consideringly. 'What other inspiring qualities does he possess?' He could see that Serena recognised the sarcasm for what it was, her lips tightening into a thin line, but she made no effort to leap to John's defence. It pleased him.

His mother took the question literally. 'He's pleasant and easy-going, and twenty-four, just the right age for Serena. They're very lucky, because John owns quite a large farm, so they won't be forced to wait if they decide to . . .'

'Well, they'll have to wait,' Adam cut incisively into his mother's enthusiasm. 'At least six months, anyway.'

'What possible reason have you for objecting?' his mother demanded with an unfamiliar stridency.

Adam narrowed his eyes and hedged the question with an unconvincing, 'She's far too young to know her own mind.'

'Whose mind—yours or hers?' Nancy used his own ammunition with a surprising vehemence, but she felt the fight was important.

Serena had sat silent throughout the increasingly heated exchange, and they had all but forgotten her presence. Her apparent calmness was all the more effective in contrast to their anger.

'If you'll excuse me, I think I'll go to bed and leave the two of you to arrange the rest of my life for me.'

Not waiting for a reaction to her quiet statement, she rose from her armchair and walked out of the room.

'Damn, damn, damn!' Adam swore softly under his breath.

Nancy went to follow Serena and then hovered uncertainly in the middle of the room. Turning back, she appealed to Adam, 'Should I go after her?'

'No, Mother,' Adam sighed heavily. There was not a doubt about the pride that had tilted that fair head. 'I think she's just about had enough of both of us for one evening.'

Nancy sank wearily down on the sofa once more, and Adam, discerning his mother's tiredness, crossed to the cabinet and poured out a glass of brandy.

'Drink this down,' Adam urged, joining her on the sofa.

Choking slightly on the spirit, Nancy muttered distraughtly, 'I didn't mean . . . I don't want to order her life like that.'

'I know, Mother, and so does Serena,' Adam was quick to reassure. He groaned when he remembered his own contribution to events. No arrogance, just a fine sense of panic when his mother had started ringing wedding bells in his ears. 'I'm sure she sees me as the villain of the piece.'

Some of his quiet despair reached Nancy.

'Adam,' she started tentatively, 'why did you say that—about not letting her marry John, I mean?'

'Because I meant it. I still do.'

'But why?'

'Why are you so anxious to see her married?' Adam hedged, but was careful to keep accusation out of his tone this time. The last thing he wanted to do was upset his mother. 'I thought you liked looking after her.'

'I do—of course I do. It's been like a new lease of life, but I won't be around for ever. I want to see her settled, and John—with John, she's . . .'

'Safe,' Adam supplied, an edge creeping back into his voice.

'There's nothing wrong with that,' Nancy protested, and made things worse with, 'John Saxon's a nice solid young man.'

And maybe Adam wanted to interpret solid as dull, but he was genuinely on Serena's side when he retorted, 'Doesn't she deserve more than that?' Only the impassioned plea left a taste of hypocrisy in his mouth, for he wanted the girl for himself and he wasn't too sure if he'd let his own unsuitability get in the way.

'Adam,' she warned, 'Serena needs security. I don't want her hurt.'

'Neither do I,' he shot back too aggressively. He was trying to make peace with his own conscience and he certainly didn't need a share in his mother's.

'Then please, Adam, stay away from her,' Nancy pleaded.

'No, I won't do that.'

'Or do you mean can't?'

'Whichever,' he muttered coldly.

'You gave me your word.'

'I promised to be polite and friendly,' he reminded her precisely. 'Well, I've been polite and now I intend to be friendly.'

'How friendly?' Nancy urged, following him as he rose.

'As friendly as she'll let me be to her.'

'Adam, I don't think she . . .' Nancy hesitated as she clutched his sleeve, 'Serena . . . I saw it tonight, but I didn't want to believe it . . . she hates you.'

Adam laughed shortly, 'Well, that's an improvement!'

'On what?'

'She told me she was completely indifferent to me.' His

eyes looked dark at the memory and he continued, fiercely, mindless of hiding anything now, 'I'd sooner she hated
me—they do say it's more akin to love.'

'No, not with this girl, not with Serena,' Nancy prayed
silently, hoping she was misreading the situation. 'Pride,
Let it be only male pride that's hurting him.'

'Is that why you're trying to spoil things between John
and her—because she hasn't fallen for you like other
women do?'

Adam was unaffected by his mother's suggestion, for
the memory of those green eyes upturned to his face willed
him to affirm his feelings. He could have lied. Afterwards
he was sorry he hadn't, but the admission rushed from
him with a cutting clarity.

'I love her, Mother . . . so much it hurts just to look at
her.'

Nancy Carmichael shook her neat silvered head from
side to side, a low moan escaping her lips. 'Because she's
so beautiful?'

'No,' Adam denied it was just sexual attraction. 'She's
more, much more than that . . .'

'No, Adam . . .' Nancy gasped, frightened by the fever
in his touch as he gripped her arms. 'She's not like that . . .
not for you, son. And I can't stand back and wait to pick
up the pieces when you've finished with her.'

'I want to marry her, Mother. Help me. Or don't stand
in my way. And if there are any broken pieces, I swear
they won't belong to Serena.'

'I can't stop you, son,' Nancy reasoned, loyalties torn in
two directions. 'You are my son and I love you, but I don't
think you and Serena could ever . . .'

Unfinished the sentence hung between them, till they
embraced, and Adam, realising the strength of his
mother's love and the nature of her dilemma, added softly,
'Neither do I, Mother, but I won't give up till *she* tells me
to.'

*

Bastard! Serena threw herself face down on the bed, thumping her pillow. Angry with herself for being stupid enough to have taken up his challenge. To have put on her loveliest dress—only to have him looking at her throughout the meal as though she was one of the courses! She had sensed those grey eyes on her and twice she had looked up, to have the impression confirmed by Adam Carmichael's steady unabashed smile. Her rude glare had only made him smile wider, and only Nancy at the head of the table stopped her from snapping his good-looking head off.

Serena rolled over and fixed her thoughts on how she could have got her own back if only they had been alone. She would have told him, in no uncertain terms, how to keep those false charms for women gullible enough to fall for them, and any possible increase in the rate of *her* heartbeat she firmly put down to the effort of suppressing her anger. He must think her a fool!

But then wasn't that just the point? Wasn't that exactly what he did think, what Andrea's will had implied—that he dictate her future?

By the time Serena had changed into her nightclothes and climbed into bed, the fury in her had died away, to be replaced by a feeling of despair whose origins lay only partly in his treatment of her as less than normal. Calm enough to hear the soft footfall outside her door, followed by a gentle knock, she was too hurt to be soothed by the muffled, 'I'm sorry, Princess,' but managed to inject some iciness into her response of, 'Go away!'

She turned her face back to seek comfort in her pillow. And although Adam knew his apology was far from adequate he was miles away from understanding the feeling behind the cold rejection, as he went back downstairs and resisted the temptation to drown his sorrows in a whisky bottle.

That afternoon he hadn't padded round her feelings, hadn't been as over-protective as the others seemed to think necessary. He hadn't treated her as a thing too delicate for emotional strain, and felt sure his abrasiveness had refreshed rather than cut. He had been a little cruel, and a lot sarcastic, but he had never doubted her ability to take it from the moment her green eyes flashed in defiance.

CHAPTER SEVEN

THE weeks passed without further incident. Despite the fact that Serena no longer made a point of missing evening meals, she either spent them looking through Adam or staring vacantly into space. Any remarks he directed at her were answered with a monosyllabic stupidity that grew irritating and then infuriating with its deliberateness. And always in the background there was Nancy, hovering like a mother hen over her chick. Six months, he gave himself. Then he would give it up. Yet deep down he knew he was lying to himself—that he would only leave the day she married someone else.

Unable to start another novel, he was totally preoccupied with her. His days were spent monitoring her movements as the long holiday from college found her painting or riding or out in his mother's specially acquired Mini— anywhere but in the house.

Adam didn't realise she was aware of his watching until one day she turned around after mounting her horse and rode up to the side terrace where he was standing.

'Why are you spying on me, Mr Carmichael?' she demanded with cold aggression.

He smiled up at her, lying smoothly, 'I didn't think I was. I like horses.'

'Then buy one,' she snapped her annoyance, 'then you won't have to watch mine all the time!'

'I just might,' he returned pleasantly, coming forward to stroke the blaze of white on the chestnut's nose. 'Will you come riding with me if I do?'

The question earned him a cold measuring look before her lips shaped derisively to offer, 'Why not?' She obviously assumed he had never been on a horse in his life and was calling his bluff. 'I'll look forward to it.'

Adam's smile broadened, as though he took her words at face value, and Serena, losing her patience with him, gathered the reins and cantered away down the rear driveway.

Three mornings later he was waiting at the entrance to the stables, wearing black jeans and polo-neck, and an old sports jacket of fawn cord.

'Good morning, Princess,' he called as she hesitated at the far end of the stable.

It brought her nearer. 'You're up early, Mr Carmichael.'

She might look like a breath of fresh air, but the hard suspicion in her voice was definitely a damper on the spirits. 'If you're trying to irritate by continually addressing me so formally, then you'll be delighted to hear you're succeeding.'

The fair head lifted a fraction higher as she claimed sullenly, 'I was taught to be respectful to my elders.'

Damn it, he wasn't *that* old! Adam thought defensively, and growled, 'Keep that up, Princess, and you just might get the spanking your childish behaviour deserves!'

'You wouldn't dare,' she flared back.

'My fingers have been itching for weeks,' he affirmed with a mock-serious tone.

Whether she recognised his threat as banter was debatable, for she countered with a vehement, 'I'm not frightened by bogeymen any more.'

'Is that how you see me?' A frown puckered her forehead and Adam gained the impression that she felt she had given something away, but her recovery was quick.

'As I rarely think about you,' she uttered disdainfully, 'I don't *see* you as anything.'

'Still indifferent, then?' he challenged softly.

'Completely.' She moved to stand directly in front of him, as though to prove it, and muttered tautly, 'Now, if you'll excuse me . . .'

He continued to bar her entrance to the stable. 'Wait a moment. I've got a surprise for you.'

'Don't you think I'm a bit old for this?' She sounded bored.

'No, I don't think so. After all, you're still young enough to show a healthy respect for your elders,' Adam replied, using her earlier sarcasm against her.

And there was frustration in her, 'Are you never lost for words?'

'Not often,' he laughed, still leaning on the stable door. Serena looked on the verge of walking off back to the house, but finally she drawled, 'Do I have to close my eyes and count to ten?'

'Only if you want to.' Adam threw his head back and laughed. Did he imagine an answering smile on her lips, quickly tightened to a grim line? Pulling his hands out of his pockets, he briefly touched her upper arms. 'Just stand there.'

He disappeared into the dim recesses of the stable, swore as he knocked over a food bucket, then re-emerged in a matter of seconds. And he didn't imagine her look of unalloyed delight as he led the white stallion into the yard; he was glad he'd given way to the crazy impulse to buy the magnificent animal.

'His name's White Lightning. Not very original, I'm afraid.'

'Can I touch him?'

The loving admiration in her eyes was almost too much for Adam; how absurd, he realised, to be jealous of a horse.

'Of course,' he matched her quiet tone.

With infinite tenderness she stroked the horse's back and then its head, all the time murmuring small nonsense words of reassurance, until the animal, recognising a potential friend, responded by nuzzling her gently with his long proud head.

'How high is he?' It was the first time she had spoken to

Adam with complete naturalness and he was nervous of causing her withdrawal.

'Sixteen hands.'

'He's beautiful,' Serena whispered with a wonder that said she was definitely not too old to be treated to surprises.

'Yes, I suppose he is.' But Adam's eyes were not on the expensive thoroughbred but staring avidly at her profile.

'Can I ride him?' she asked, appeal brightening her voice and the green eyes turned towards him.

Adam cursed himself for his stupidity in not foreseeing the possibility. If he didn't allow her on the horse, they would be back to square one, but there was no way he was going to chance her breaking her beautiful neck.

'I'm afraid not, Princess.' Immediately her change of expression told him the spell cast by White Lightning was broken.

'Why not?' she quizzed.

'He's too big for you,' Adam trod softly.

'I'm not scared,' she pursued, 'and I am a good rider.'

'Look, I have grave doubts about handling him myself, far less a little thing like you.'

Serena totally missed the tenderness in his voice and her own was vibrant with anger. 'Congratulations, Mr Carmichael!' she snapped.

'For what?' he frowned.

'I think you know.'

Her tone struck him like a blow to the stomach; she actually believed he had deliberately taunted her with the horse to gain some malicious pleasure in refusing to let her ride it! Sometimes he wondered why he bothered with this girl who was glaring fiercely back at him. She was prickly, unforgiving, and quite often downright rude. If someone had asked him right at that moment, Miss Serena Jane Templeton didn't deserve *him*!

'Don't move!' he shouted down at her.

When he returned with the saddle over his arm, he was

surprised to find she hadn't. Deftly he strapped the leather to the animal's back. In one fluid movement he mounted, and before Serena could guess what was in his mind, he stretched down and adroitly hoisted her on to the saddle in front of him.

'Put me down!' she commanded, her body going rigid.

'Shut up and hang on, or so help me, I'll land you on your backside in the mud!' She gasped, opening her mouth to protest, and he forestalled her with, 'And yes, I would dare.'

He eased her into a more comfortable position, then gently pulled her back so she was forced to lean against him for support, before spurring the horse on. Even with two riders on its back, the horse was strong and fast, and when they reached open countryside Adam gave it its head. He wasn't sure if his sense of exhilaration was caused by the horse's speed or the small warm body curved into his.

He took the direction she silently indicated, then almost spilled off when they went through a small patch of low-branched trees at the base of a long sloping hill, ducking his head just in time. He felt her shake with suppressed laughter and squeezed her hard as punishment. So Serena had a taste for danger as well as speed!

At the top of the hill he reined in the horse. Reckoning that they were about four miles away from the house—and too far away for her to walk back—he lowered her gently to the ground, then slid off the saddle.

Her hair tumbled in golden waves as she removed her riding hat. She was breathless and excited from the ride—and it hurt just to look at her.

'You're crazy,' she managed to articulate between breaths, but there was no malice in her words.

'Why?'

'Heredity, I suppose,' she quipped, her mouth quirking at the corners while the pleasure of the ride still lingered.

'You're quite a wit, Princess,' Adam smiled.

There was no mistaking the underlying bitterness in her snappy reply of, 'Well, that's an improvement on being considered half that quantity!'

'Don't!' He caught her by the arm.

'Don't what?' Confused by his urgency, she stayed her ground.

'We were almost having a conversation. Don't spoil it!' Adam understood full well Serena's behaviour over the previous fortnight; he needed to get through to her. 'At my mother's request, I went to my aunt's funeral. Up until the reading of her will, where you gave a convincing performance of being exactly as Andrea stated, I'd never heard of you. I admit I considered following the course she suggested, and maybe that's why she chose me as your guardian—because I was just hard enough to take the easy option and tidy you away in some institution without too many qualms.' He still held her interest, but it was difficult to read more from her expression. 'But from the first time you spoke to me, I have never viewed you as in any way mentally deficient—quite the opposite, in fact. You were confused, yes, and maybe a little wild in your thinking, but I suspect your experience with Andrea gave you the right to be.'

Serena ignored the half-question in his last remark, but seemed to be reflecting on what he had been saying, her eyes staring into space. Or maybe she was playing dumb again? Adam exerted a slight pressure on her arm.

'You advised Nancy to consult a psychiatrist, didn't you?'

Was it an accusation?—difficult to judge from the cool eyes trained on him once more.

'You needed help, Princess,' he gave the truth gently, but she was an agonisingly long time in coming back with a barely audible Yes. It was a start. 'Maybe Simon Clarke turned out to be a bad choice, mm?'

'He helped a little,' she conceded warily, 'but he was a bit . . . disappointing.'

In what way disappointing? Adam speculated, but
Serena moved away before he could press the point. Had
she resented the personal interest his mother had hinted at
in a letter? Or rejected Simon when he had failed to accept
her revelations about the past at face value?

Serena had wandered off towards a fallen tree. Adam
followed and sat down beside her, taking a packet of
cigarettes and lighter from his jacket. Lighting one, he
inhaled deeply; he hadn't felt this nervous since his first
date with a girl.

'It's beautiful.' His hand swept the valley, rural England at its best, haphazard and rich with colour.

'Yes . . . yes, it is,' she stammered.

Serena was coping with her own tension as Adam failed
to live up to the image she had given him.

'Have you painted it?' he asked tentatively.

'My . . . my father did,' she admitted falteringly, and on
impulse added, 'And he did it too well for any effort of
mine to stand comparison . . . my own standards, I mean.'

Adam nodded his understanding, but he felt he had to
give a little in order to receive any confidence. Not quite
truthfully he confessed, 'My own father was a financial
genius. I admired and loved him a lot, but in the end I
couldn't follow him. Much to my family's disgust I dropped out of my economics course at Cambridge and have
held the dubious honour of black sheep ever since.'

'That's not fair!' Her vehemence startled both of them,
and Serena stammered under his searching appraisal, 'I
mean what you do . . . your writing, it's more important
than making money. Creating something for other people
to enjoy.'

The defensive gleam lingered in her eyes and warmed
him, even while he forced himself not to make anything
out of it.

He teased her seriousness with a wry,' Even if it's
creating sensational garbage?' She dropped her eyes
away, and bending closer, Adam discerned colour flood-

ing her high slanting cheekbones—totally unexpected,
utterly entrancing when he intuitively determined its
origin. Fleetingly he touched her face with the back of
his hand and she swayed rather than jerked back from
him.

'Delightful though it is, your blush is unwarranted,
Princess. Perhaps if you'd been around with your re-
freshingly candid opinion, I wouldn't have sunk to such
depths. But depths they were, and if anyone should be
embarrassed by that film script, it's the writer.'

The frank admission brought Serena's head up to catch
the self-derision curving his mouth. His books, clever and
articulate, had more than suggested that the writer was
not enamoured with the human race, but she had been
wrong in assuming that Adam Carmichael held himself in
any higher esteem.

'But if you knew, then why . . .' she trailed off in her
confusion.

'A joke on the black side that backfired,' he murmured
obscurely. But when she still waited, her small head
upturned to his, he tried to enlighten her without
broaching on self-pity. 'Imagine you do a painting, a
gallery dismissed it as non-commercial, and in a fit of
artistic pique you alter it to the sort of bargain basement
print that makes you cringe. And guess what happens?'

'They love it.' Serena's rueful smile held sympathy as
she followed the analogy, but her, 'I would have destroyed
it,' was emphatic.

Adam had no answer for the youthful certainty confronting him. He looked away from her, his eyes travelling
the valley.

And Serena, sensing his sudden remoteness, was more
than a little baffled by her reaction to it. She felt shut out
and strangely resentful.

'Why did you pretend in your letters that you liked
Hollywood?' she asked bluntly, almost demanding his
attention.

He did nothing about the hardness in his voice as he replied, 'It's a habit that grows on people round my dear mother—keeping her in the dark about the less savoury parts of one's life. Only some of us are more adept at it than others, aren't we?' he finished on a sardonic note, then instantly regretted it as she made a move to rise.

Serena gave up the uneven struggle to prise his fingers from around her arm and tried to disguise her hurt under a biting defensive reply of, 'You're full of clever remarks, aren't you?'

But it reached Adam and made him feel sick with himself as he groaned quietly, 'I'm a blundering fool, aren't I?' His apology was received with an ambiguous silence, confusion warring with suspicion. Neither was encouraging, and Adam knew if he had any sense he would leave it there. He hadn't. 'Look, Serena, I didn't mean that the way it sounded. I understand your motives for hiding things from my mother—I've done it for years myself—but you don't have to do it with me. I want to help you.'

'Help?' she repeated stiffly. His sudden return to gentleness was a trap. It had to be, so why was she waiting for it to spring? 'What things am I hiding?'

'You tell me, Princess,' said Adam very quietly, slowly releasing his hold on her arm. Pressure would not work. Her face was very still and unreadable. 'About Andrea.'

Yesterday she wouldn't even have wanted to believe the sensitivity she could see in his face, far less be tempted by it. She had to keep looking through him, not at him.

'Andrea . . .' She fixed her eyes on a point past his left shoulder. 'Andrea who?'

For a second Adam could have shaken her, but it passed under the certainty that behind the blank evasion there lay scars, as yet unhealed. Was he right to touch their rawness? He didn't know.

Serena didn't resist as he laid the palm of his hand lightly against her cheek to bring her into the direct line of his vision, but then she didn't seem to be registering his presence any more. He tried anyway, a quiet thread of persistence running through his tone.

'OK, I'll tell you what I know. A few years after your mother's death, your father decides to return to England. He meets Andrea—a childless widow in her forties. They seem suited. Only where your father is thinking of a companion and mother for you, Andrea is looking for more than just affection.'

'He tried!' Serena burst out, eyes flaring with indignation, unable to let the implied criticism pass. 'My father was kind and patient, but nothing he did ever satisfied *your* aunt!'

There were overtones of the child Serena in her angry defence: and like a child where she loved, she did so passionately. Adam wondered how his aunt had killed that spirit.

'Including getting rid of your beautiful mother's portrait,' he said at last. 'Your mother *was* very beautiful. And your father loved her. Perhaps far too much for a second marriage to be wise. And my aunt was jealous —all that wouldn't be easy for a young orphan to understand, Princess.'

As an attempt at reasoning through the past it was well off the mark, for Serena struck his hand angrily away.

'You know nothing about it!'

'Then tell me,' he demanded, rising with her, as she jumped up.

'*Your* aunt was a devouring monster!' she practically screamed before rudely turning her back on him.

Adam felt desperate and reached out to spin her round towards him. He sounded harsh. 'You're never going to forgive me either, are you, for being related to Andrea?'

'No—no, I'm not!' Serena cried wildly, more out of chaos than reason as his hands tightened round her middle. Through the anger and bitterness broke a clamouring excitement at the spreading of his fingers on the flat of her stomach, crazily out of place in her feelings for him. 'You're hurting me, you brute!' she lied.

'Then stop struggling like a wildcat. Look at me!' he ordered, his own control slipping fast. With one arm he pulled her closer, trapping her arms against his chest, and his other hand tangled in her fine hair, forcing her to obey him. 'What do you see?' he muttered tensely, sure that his features must be betraying his feelings for her.

'I see six foot two of pure arrogance!' Serena sneered recklessly, recognising only the hard male desire that burned in his eyes. 'Is that how you get turned on, Adam Carmichael—showing off your strength to defenceless women?'

'You blind little fool,' Adam murmured deep in his throat. 'I don't want to hurt you. I just want to . . .'

The lips, hard and searching, tried to articulate his emotion, for he was beyond words. A great hunger worked up inside him, but his need to deepen the kiss was thwarted by her clenched teeth, and he growled in his frustration, 'Open your mouth.' Her angry protest was stifled as he took advantage of it. The taste of her was sweet and intoxicating, causing the blood to surge to his brain, and miraculously the mouth under his began to move, tentatively answering his. He sensed her inexperience and the nature of his kiss changed, his lips gentle and persuasive as they sought to give reassurance as well as pleasure. Unprepared for even this shy response, his senses stirred unbearably. He started to draw away, but lost the good intention in her arms slowly stretching upwards to pull his mouth closer, asking for more while they trembled nervously in anticipation of it.

But even with Serena straining on tiptoe and Adam bending to meet her, the kiss satisfied neither, and encircling her waist, he raised her till she was level with his mouth, bracing her slight body against his. And what Serena lacked in experience, she made up for in instinct as she brushed her quivering mouth tantalisingly against his

until hard male lips once more claimed hers, absorbing
and draining her sweetness.

It was a kiss Adam was to relive long after he lowered
her gently to the ground, unable to take much more of her
nearness. While some notion of decency was still remaining, he set the girl in his arms abruptly away from him,
and felt crippled by the look in her eyes at his roughness.

'Try to understand. I had to stop while I was still able
to.'

His appeal went unheard. Her lovely face was a mirror
of her feelings as the hurt at his supposed rejection
struggled with a deep shame at her own abandoned
response to his lovemaking.

Clinging to the belief that the perfect passion they had
shared must have burned down the barriers between
them, Adam put his arms out automatically to gather her
protectively to him, and was caught unprepared for the
violence of her reaction as she shoved him with all her
strength. By the time he had regained his balance, mental
and physical, she was running from him towards White
Lightning. She had untied the reins loosely looped over
the branch of a tree and was heaving herself up into the
saddle before her intentions came fully home to him.

'Get off the horse, Serena!' Panic made his voice hard,
as the horse skittered, nervous of the sudden movement;
Adam placed himself in front of it, regardless of the very
real danger of the horse shying and catching him a blow
with its rearing hooves. 'You'll break your neck!'

'As if you'd care!' The broken cry made her sound
young and painfully vulnerable.

Making soothing noises to the horse, Adam quietened
the animal sufficiently to come alongside, ready to grab
the reins when he could. Inching his hand up the stallion's
long neck, he entreated softly, 'Get down, Princess,
please,' as he recognised and gained a measure of relief
from the flickering doubt in her eyes.

He had almost reached the bridle when Serena brought

her leg out and kicked him back from the horse, and whether by accident or design he was sent sprawling on the muddy ground.

He watched her gallop down the hill, her hair streaming in the wind, making no attempt to slow the horse's progress when they reached the belt of trees, and his fear for her fought his respect for her fearlessness.

It took him a bare forty minutes to cover the four miles back to the house, and he was almost choked with the relief of finding White Lightning back in his stall, quietly munching a well-deserved breakfast. It quickly turned to anger when he was confronted by the old gardener, patently struggling to conceal his amusement at the master's mud-splattered appearance.

'Had a bit of an accident . . . sir?'

'You could say that. Where's Miss Templeton?' Adam demanded with grim impatience.

But Brocklehurst, enjoying what he accurately assumed to be the situation, was slow in answering, 'Miss Serena's gone to t'house.'

'Has the animal been rubbed down?'

'That he has, sir. Beautiful animal, but very strong,' the old man muttered, running a fond eye over the muscular flesh, before offering another unsolicited but definite opinion. 'Begging your pardon, sir, but if I were you I wouldn't let young miss ride 'im too often.'

'I don't intend to.' The disapproval in the other's voice made Adam clench his teeth. 'I'd better go and change.'

'Aye, 'tis muddy out after last night's storm,' Fred Brocklehurst commented, and because he was fond of a bit of harmless mischief, added, ''Twas surprised when young miss told me you wanted to walk back.'

Adam could not trust himself to speak and walked away before the gardener could glimpse the thunder in his expression which would have had the old man hastily revising the word harmless. Fury carried him across the and up the stairs, but instead of going to his room

Adam made for the west wing, not bothering to wait for a response to his peremptory knock. He firmly closed the door behind him, and it said much for his swift reactions that he missed the flying hairbrush that greeted his arrival.

'Temper, temper,' he drawled, leaning negligently against the door. He wasn't going to let the girl turn him inside out—not this time.

Swivelling completely round from the dressing table, Serena hurled her next barrage verbally. 'If you're not out of my room in one minute I shall scream the house down!'

'Stop being so hysterical,' he summarily dismissed the threat, folding his arms. 'You're fully clothed . . . unfortunately.'

'If you'd come in a couple of minutes ago,' she retorted blushingly, 'I wouldn't have been.'

'In that case I'll have to run quicker, Princess,' he returned smoothly,' the next time you decide I'm in need of exercise.'

It disconcerted her. Serena had expected him to be mad, but then she had also been confident of being away from the house long before he arrived back. He must have run all the way—but why? Not to treat her with this lazy indulgence, she was sure.

'You have thirty seconds to leave before I start scream-ing,' she muttered tightly, getting to her feet.

Adam adopted an even more casual stance that implied he had no intention of quitting the room and made Serena clench her fingers.

'Twenty seconds . . .'

'As my mother appears to be out,' Adam continued with light mockery, 'I can only assume the outraged virgin act is to be performed for the benefit of the owner of the Range Rover parked outside.'

'Ten seconds,' she warned coldly, her glare showing she was just as angry as he was below the surface.

'Are you sure you want to want to risk a fight between

the young man and myself? The wrong person might get hurt,' he suggested, an amused edge to his voice.

'I doubt it,' Serena retorted with heavy insult that didn't seem to make any impression at all.

'Will you bathe my wounds, Princess?' Adam bantered back. 'It might be worth getting a black eye.'

'Don't be ridiculous!'

'Your deadline is up,' Adam smiled, uncrossing his arms to theatrically place a finger in each ear. 'Scream away.'

'Oh, stop being so silly!' she shouted her exasperation, no defence ready against this playful side of Adam Carmichael. She gave way to impulse, and covering the space between them, ungraciously dragged his hands away from his head.

With a neat twist, Adam literally gained the upper hand and, lips twisting, asked, 'Have you screamed?'

'You damn well know I haven't!' Serena snapped, failing to free her hands from his.

She went very still and lowered her eyes, but Adam wasn't foiled, for the pulse at her wrist was hammering furiously. He brought her back to him by remarking wryly, 'I'm sincerely touched that you couldn't bear to watch me being beaten to within an inch of my life, as the expression goes.'

'If you continue making infuriating remarks,' she shot back, 'I might change my mind!'

'I don't think so, Serena,' Adam murmured, no longer convinced it was all temper in her flashing eyes.

'I wouldn't bet on it!'

'No, I don't think I'd ever be so foolish as to lay money on how you would react to anything,' he conceded, shedding his air of amusement. 'Take that kiss we shared, for instance . . .'

'Shut up!' Tinges of red appeared on her cheeks.

'There's nothing to be ashamed of in enjoying a kiss, Princess,' he warned quite seriously.

'I didn't!' she denied hotly.

'That's not what that sensuous mouth of yours was telling me,' he reminded her ruthlessly, his gaze moving to her lips now covered with a light gloss. 'Perhaps we should put it to the test again.'

It had her backing away. 'If you do, I'll . . .'

'Scream? We seem to be going round in circles, don't you think?' said Adam with heavy patience, dropping his hold on her. 'Let's take it as read that you won't scream and I won't kiss you unless either of us is provoked.'

'What do you want from me?' she demanded, the arrogant tilt of her golden head a provocation in itself.

'I'm surprised you haven't worked that out yet,' he replied cryptically, and received a glare of contempt that told him Serena had put her own interpretation on his interest in her. He narrowed his eyes to it and forced himself to say, 'But no matter, Princess, the light will dawn one day,' in a lighter manner. 'An apology will do for now.'

'An apology?' she cried disbelievingly. 'For what?'

Adam wanted to say for causing him one of the worst half hours of his life when he had feared to find her unconscious body every step of the way back, but his pride wouldn't let him. Instead he stated coldly, 'For giving me two bruised ribs, should be sufficient reason.'

'You're . . . you're mad,' Serena gasped, 'if you think I'm going to say I'm sorry for something I would do again without hesitation!'

'A rather savage reaction to a kiss, wouldn't you say?' he muttered insinuatingly, for he had taken more than enough of her defiance.

But Serena was thinking along similar lines. Adam really was insufferable! One more sarcastic remark about that kiss, and she felt she would hit him. She knew she would. And catching the sardonic gleam in his eyes as they travelled over the rapid rise and fall of her breasts, she almost did.

Adam watched her retreat to the bed and snatch up the jacket of her stylish skirt suit—a picture of controlled fury. She was sending him a little crazy, he realised, for he had actually wanted her to hit him—a token of hate if she wouldn't give him anything else?

And she had reverted to icy indifference when confronting him once more. 'If you'll excuse me, I have a guest waiting downstairs.'

'We'll go down together, shall we?' said Adam with mock pleasantness.

'No!' she snapped, the speed and harshness of her refusal supporting the idea that she was acutely anxious to keep the two men apart.

'Oh, but I've been looking forward to meeting your fiancé,' he baited, leaning back on the door as she took a step towards it.

'He's not!' she denied hotly—and then wondered why she had rejected the one relationship that even a cynic like Adam Carmichael might just respect.

'That sounded like pure panic to me.' Adam smiled, his satisfaction purring. 'Why are you so bothered about my meeting the worthy John?'

'I'm not,' Serena returned quickly, but his knowing smile sparked off her temper again. 'OK, *Mr* Carmichael, you've asked for it. John Saxon is an extremely amiable, kind and gentle person—' She paused, faltering slightly, but gathered resolve from his lazy posture. She dragged out each word. 'Whereas you are, without doubt, the most conceited, detestable, nasty . . .'

Adam cut her off mid-sentence. 'Skip it, Princess, I can get the message.'

And he left Serena staring dumbfounded as the door closed behind him. She'd hurt him. She'd actually got through his tough male hide and inflicted the pain that had darkened and then shut his eyes in a moment's anguish before he had slammed out of the room. It made no sense. Nothing did any more—not his erratic behaviour, nor her chaotic response to it. She had wanted to hurt him. She had been unbelievably successful. He deserved it. So why should she go running to him to seek forgiveness?

'There you are,' John Saxon called up with mild impatience, halting Serena midflight at the top of the stairs. 'Have you forgotten me?' he teased, with no suspicion that his laughing surmise was literally true. 'Come on, darling, you're always worth waiting for, but this time we're very, very late.'

The light male laughter carried up to Adam's room. Furiously he tore off his mud-splattered clothing, cursing and wanting her with each alternate breath. Images of strangling her with his bare hands were inextricably mixed with the vision of making love to her between cool white sheets that made him ache in the pit of his stomach. He heard the front door open and close—and lost the battle to keep away from the window.

Just before she climbed into her seat Serena leaned forward and startled John by kissing him with a force and urgency he could neither understand nor answer. She drew back, and smiled, shielding the disappointment that the earth was never going to move with nice kind John. When she turned from him her eyes, cool and passionless, lifted of their own accord and she stared without surprise at the man framed in one of the long windows. Her gaze was steady and betrayed none of the growing fear that no matter how much she disliked him, Adam Carmichael might spoil her for any other man.

And Adam looked on, seeing the kiss as brutal retaliation for his own and the mockery in her beautiful upturned face as the continued twisting of the knife with which she had already cut him. His fist slammed full force into the wall, blood trickling unheeded from his knuckles.

CHAPTER EIGHT

A GLANCE at the catalogue told him that the item in which he was specifically interested was about to be sold. It was the third auction he had attended in Yorkshire, and he had been pleasantly surprised by the wealth of treasures to be found. Today he was determined to buy a painting.

He had seen it at the preview, and despite its uninspiring description—mother and child by unknown artist—he had at once recognised both its origin and subject.

Normally Adam set himself a limit above which he resisted the temptation to continue bidding; this time, however, he was prepared to bid until he got what he wanted, regardless of price.

The bidding started sluggishly, with the auctioneer chiding the crowd for their reluctance to make an offer for what he called a very nice little painting, a description which made Adam cringe. Initially the bidding was between a rather plump woman sitting just in front of Adam, and a voice coming from the back of the large manor hall where the sale was taking place.

Adam relaxed, waiting for the moment he thought fit to enter the auction. The price had settled round the five hundred mark when a man on the sidelines overstepped it by one hundred. Adam intuitively recognised him as a dealer. The plump woman who had wanted to take the cute little painting back to her home in Nebraska dropped out, her husband having announced in an over-loud whisper that 'it wasn't that cute'. The dealer and the voice from the back continued competing until the bidding rose to over two thousand pounds. The expression on the auctioneer's face plainly revealed his dismay at having missed out on something by not bringing in a valuer—it had already gone too high for the work of an unknown. Again the bidding stabilised, this time at two and a half thousand pounds, with the dealer's offer highest.

Adam fractionally lifted his hand at the words 'going once', indicating his bid of three and a half. His large jump was intended to discourage competition. It did not succeed, because the dealer came back with an offer improved by five hundred pounds, his thinking the same as Adam's. For eight thousand pounds it eventually became Adam's property, and he suffered with a smile of satisfaction the curious stares of the American couple before the auction recommenced.

The final lots disposed of, he presented his cheque at the auctioneer's table and arranged for delivery of the painting. His good mood did not, however, last, for as he threaded his way through the crowd round the table, he caught sight of a familiar figure at the back of the hall.

Serena stood alone, hanging back from the man she was with as he became involved in a conversation with another couple. Something in her stance told Adam she was aware of his presence and avoiding his stare.

They had not exchanged a word for a fortnight, but this time of silence had not been initiated by Serena. The first few days after their last encounter had left Adam too bruised and battle-weary to do anything but keep well away from her. Since then he had discovered why anyone she associated with Andrea was treated to such passionate dislike, and because he felt she must want him gone—but was too proud to say so—he knew he should think of leaving Yorkshire—and sooner rather than later.

And he would have left the auction without going near her if she hadn't looked round at him making his way to the exit and acknowledged him by quickly averting her head.

Starved for contact, Adam couldn't help approaching her, and when he saw her back stiffen as she sensed his intention, he prepared to don the mask he had come to use to disguise his feelings.

'What a coincidence,' he said, striving for a friendliness that was immediately interpreted as sarcasm.

'Isn't it just?' she replied icily, flicking him a sideways glance that was anything but welcoming.

'It is actually.' He hesitated and found himself lost for something neutral to say. With each of them tense and silent he had just determined to walk away . . .

'Aren't you going to introduce us, Serena?' John Saxon had finished his conversation with the other couple whose drifting away had brought his attention back to her.

'John,' she stammered,' this is Adam Carmichael . . . my step-cousin . . .'

Both men waited for her to complete the formality, and Adam, realising she didn't intend to, quickly greeted the younger man, 'How do you do? I've been so looking forward to meeting you.'

'I'm afraid you have the advantage of me, Mr Carmichael. Serena hasn't . . .' John Saxon broke off uneasily.

'I quite understand. Our little Serena has failed to mention my existence,' Adam bantered lightly, driven on by the severe chill wafting in his direction. 'Or perhaps you know me better as the wicked guardian.'

At this the young farmer looked even more uncomfortable. 'I wasn't aware that Serena had a guardian,' he eventually managed, more mystified than annoyed at the knowledge he had gained as he gave Serena a puzzled frown. 'Why didn't you tell me, darling?'

'Don't look so hurt, John. He's just teasing.' Serena's eyes shifted to Adam, daring him to contradict her, and on a note of accusation, she added, 'My step-cousin loves to tease.'

'Oh, I see. It was a joke.' John did not understand the supposed humour, but he looked relieved by her assurance. 'Pleased to meet you, Mr Carmichael.'

Adam was also perplexed, too puzzled to deny Serena's

assertion. Surely she had at least mentioned his existence—even if only as an obstruction to their plans?

'We'd better go, John,' she pressed, touching his arm.

'Plenty of time, darling,' said John, still curious and completely missing her anxiety.

Adam didn't. 'If you and Serena have to hurry off somewhere . . .'

'Oh no, not in the least,' John interrupted. 'It's sort of an afternoon off for me, coming to a sale.'

'Did you get what you wanted?' Adam was making conversation, sensing that Serena was on the verge of another request to depart.

'Yes, some farm machinery—good condition too,' John enthused, oblivious of the tension surrounding him, 'but Serena wasn't quite so lucky.'

'Oh, and what were you after, Princess?' Adam asked pleasantly, the nickname slipping out as he tried to improve the atmosphere between them.

'It doesn't matter.' The set of her chin told him she was determined not to be drawn.

'Serena's a bit disappointed,' John rushed to defend her show of moodiness. 'I was bidding for a painting she liked but—well, it suddenly took off, and Serena agreed with me, it would have been sheer stupidity to carry on,' the younger man explained, and becoming increasingly uncomfortable under Adam's steady gaze, justified himself with, 'Not that I couldn't afford it or anything, but a painting is just a painting, after all, unless it's by somebody famous. Then, of course, it's an investment.'

Adam shuddered inwardly at such a Philistine notion and Serena's eyes, threatening and narrowed, reflected her awareness of his thoughts. How could she contemplate marrying someone who did not share even a passing interest in her world?

'Another coincidence,' Adam murmured dryly. 'I think we may have been after the same painting.'

'Good lord!' John exclaimed. 'Were you the late bidder seated near the front?'

'The same,' Adam nodded.

'Did you get it?' John enquired curiously. 'I missed the closing bid.'

'He gets everything he sets his mind to, don't you?' It was Serena's first voluntary contribution to the conversation and it was no compliment.

'Almost everything, Princess,' Adam calmly answered the bitter reproach, although it hurt as it was meant to. 'In the case of the painting, my patience was rewarded. But some things don't come quite so easily.'

'But then anything that doesn't,' Serena declared stonily, 'you don't find much difficulty in shrugging off, do you?'

She was now positively glowering at him and for a second Adam just stared at her, scarcely believing the undercurrents he was picking up from the acid remark. The contrary creature was piqued that he had been ignoring her.

'I believe you've just renewed my interest,' Adam matched her cryptic note, feeling, rightly or wrongly, suddenly free of any obligation to stay away from her, and waited her reaction.

But John, who had been standing on the sidelines of the exchange, not surprisingly lost as to its subject and made to feel an unwanted third, put his arm round Serena's shoulders and cut in with, 'You must have wanted it awfully badly to pay that sort of money for an apparently worthless painting.'

'Did you think it worthless, Mr Saxon?' Adam switched his attention back to the other man, pinning him down with a cold, challenging stare.

'John,' he offered his more familiar name, although he seemed uncertain of his words before Serena's more mature cousin, 'I admit it was pretty, but as a business proposition . . .'

'Your accountant wouldn't approve,' Adam finished it for him, neatly and damningly.

The sarcasm was totally missed as John gave a selfconscious laugh before conceding, 'He'd have a fit.'

'And what value would you put on it, Serena?' Adam baited.

'I think you know,' she returned coolly, moving closer into the circle of John's arm, to irritate, Adam was sure, for as a protector, John was proving himself severely inadequate.

He looked confused, late to catch up with their near-antagonist attitude towards each other. 'I am a bit at sea. Was there something special about the painting, darling?'

Adam forestalled her automatic denial. 'You could say that. It's by Graham Templeton, Serena's father, and I would say, judging by the age of the child model and her present age, it was painted about fourteen years ago. Am I right?'

'I can't remember,' she snapped.

'You haven't changed much. Well, in the face anyway,' Adam murmured, eyes moving over her feminine curves: the little girl playing beside her mother on a sandy beach had not worn any clothing.

John's slight opening of his mouth registered belated understanding. 'You should have told me, Serena. If I'd known . . .' he stuttered helplessly.

How the young man had failed to recognise Serena in the beautiful golden child or her present likeness to the mother, lovingly painted by the artist, was a wonder to Adam, but he refrained from saying so. He could not, however, resist the temptation to add to his palpable discomfort.

'You would have gone on in the bidding?'

'Yes, of course. If it means a lot to Serena,' he blustered and overcoming with marked hesitation the parsimony instilled by his late father continued, 'Perhaps you will consider letting me buy it from you.'

'John, it doesn't matter. Really it doesn't,' Serena urged quickly, guessing at what Adam was trying to achieve. She pulled at John's sleeve. 'Didn't you say you had to go and check on the loading of the machinery?'

'Golly, yes,' John agreed, glancing at his watch and showing himself remarkably simple to distract. 'You're a treasure for reminding me. Perhaps Mr Carmichael will look after you while I go and do it.'

'Oh no, John!' Serena's protest was too vehement, and realising how strange it must sound, she hastily improvised, 'Adam's too busy, aren't you?' Her expression, hidden from her escort, held dire warnings of the consequences of accepting John's tentative suggestion.

But it served as a challenge to Adam, who came back smoothly, 'Not at all. I'd be delighted.' He smiled disarmingly at a hesitant John. 'You run off and look after your combine harvester and I'll take care of Serena . . . for you.'

'Baler, actually,' John laughed nervously, and when Serena failed to voice any more objections, reassured her, 'I won't be long, darling. See you soon.'

The moment the younger man was out of earshot, the inevitable explosion occurred. 'What in hell's name do you think you're doing, Mr Carmichael?'

'It was Adam a few minutes ago,' he recalled musingly, maddeningly calm in the face of the anger flaring to life in the eyes upturned to his. 'Does the worthy John know his prospective bride has such a fiery temper—not to mention such unladylike language?'

'Don't try to distract me,' she seethed.

'That tactic seems very effective as far as the boyfriend's concerned,' Adam continued in the same vein.

'What do you mean?'

'From art to farm machinery in one fluid movement,' he commented, his mouth lifting at the corners with a suspicion of amusement. 'Very manageable—or perhaps he wanted a let out?'

'Are you trying to imply that John was avoiding making you an offer for the painting,' she fumed, hands on the hips of her black dungarees, 'because if you were . . .'

'Nothing was further from my mind,' Adam lied outrageously, raising his hands in submission to her warlike stance. 'However, we'll let him vindicate himself, if you like. I'll let him have the painting for, say,' he paused for mental calculation, 'eight and a half thousand.'

'Quite the wheeler-dealer, aren't we?' she muttered with heavy contempt, not realising she was being played with.

'Not particularly. I could get a lot more for it in a London gallery. Anyway it's purely academic,' Adam murmured pacifyingly, but his smile was met with hard hostility. Certainly no invitation to offer the truth. She'd be looking for the twist, and probably finding one, two seconds after he admitted he had bought the painting to return to its rightful owner. Instead he said, 'I don't think the money will be forthcoming.'

Said to gain reaction and he was suitably rewarded with a taunting, 'John may not flaunt it, but he could buy you several times over, I bet.'

'I doubt it, Princess,' Adam responded unruffled. 'Is that why you consider him such good husband material— because he's rich and . . . careful?'

'No, it isn't!' she almost shouted her denial, not missing the slur that translated 'careful' into 'mean'.

'Then why?' he wanted to know. He could hardly say what was in his mind—what's he got that I haven't got?

But perhaps Serena partially homed into his thoughts, or maybe it was her struggling to maintain her defiance, anger out of stride with his reasonable tone, that made her state defensively, 'He's a better man than you'll ever be.'

'In a certain sense I would not deny that,' Adam concurred, now having to keep his own temper on a tight leash while she trampled over his pride. 'He's kind, tractable, polite and incredibly dull, I should imagine.

Have I missed out any of his more sterling qualities?' he
jibed knowingly, and for a split second the widening of her
eyes, spitting fury and frustration, made him think the
whole hall—auctioneer, helpers and few remaining cus-
tomers waiting to settle—were about to hear her answer,
loud and reverberatingly angry.

She visibly swallowed it down and caught him off
balance as she drew very close to him, waited till he
inclined his head slightly and then whispered confidingly,
'He's also fantastic in bed!'

The knife turned another inch and he felt physically ill.
His hands went out to painfully grip her upper arms
before she could walk away with her victory, and for a
moment as the blood hammering in his head blotted out
reason, there was a very real danger that Adam would be
the one to supply a public scene.

As his vision cleared, he was rescued by the sight of
Serena biting down on her bottom lip. Sliding his hold to
one wrist, he pulled her behind him, out of the house,
across the courtyard until they were well out of range of
anyone else's hearing at the top of a short flight of steps
leading down to the front lawn. And there he backed her
against a stone parapet.

'I don't believe you!' Adam sounded menacing, a bare
step from violence as he dared her to repeat her assertion.

But she dared, and perhaps she wouldn't have been the
girl he loved if she hadn't, returning flippantly, 'Do you
want details?'

'I was not referring to your milk-and-water boy-friend's
prowess as a lover,' he ground out, winding her hair round
one hand and tugging hard. 'I don't believe that my virgin
princess in her little-girl dungarees has ever lain with a
man, far less had violent, passionate love made to her.'

'I couldn't care less what you think,' she cried back,
colour flushing her cheeks that could have been down to
temper or embarrassment. 'My *affairs* are my own concern!'

She gave the word affairs a meaning that made him once again wish to strike her. He yanked her head further back and growled, 'You'd better be lying!' and any girl with a fainter spirit would have recognised it as a demand for her to shut up, as was the pressure with which her hair was gripped.

If Serena Templeton recognised it, she chose to ignore, coming back with a reckless, 'That's for me to know.'

'Finish it!' he ordered, but this time she stared uncomprehendingly up at him; only Adam felt she knew exactly what she was doing to him—more than teasing but a fine instinct for torment. 'Presumably for me to find out, eh? Well, don't worry, I promise I shall.'

He caught her hand as it was in mid-air about to make vicious contact with his face, releasing his grip on her hair. What her next move would have been he wasn't to find out, for they were separated by the tooting of a horn as John spotted them from his Range Rover. For an instant her resentment appeared to switch to the source of the interruption before she sprang back from him.

'You look disappointed,' Adam tested the impression she had given, before she managed to erect her guard. 'Perhaps you have a taste for fighting.'

'Don't be absurd!' she snapped back, but without her usual force or conviction. Her next words, as near to appeal as she had ever come, seemed to suggest an embarrassed guilt.

'If . . . if John saw us, if he says anything, we were . . . fooling, right?'

'I wasn't fooling,' said Adam with quiet warning, as her attention wavered nervously between himself and John, alighting from the Rover with a female passenger. 'Nevertheless your wish is my command, Princess.'

His half-bow earned him a withering glance, but she submitted to his guiding hand at her elbow as they went forward to meet John, Adam taking notice of the younger man's companion with an admiring, 'Who's your competition? She's quite a dish!'

'I think she approves of you too,' Serena commented with acid sweetness on the encouraging smile turned on by the other girl for Adam's benefit as they approached.

The smile slipped as the brunette acknowledged Serena, purring, 'Delighted to see you, Serena. What a pretty playsuit so sweet!'

The compliment, so innocent at face value, served to draw attention, by contrast, to her own more mature figure and style of dress—an elegant, well-cut trouser suit. With bold features, highlighted by carefully applied make-up, she might once have appealed to Adam.

'This is Serena's cousin—Adam Carmichael. Adam, a next-door neighbour of mine—Caroline Stamford,' John diffidently performed the introductions.

'Naughty Serena,' Caroline murmured playfully, stretching a beautifully manicured hand out to Adam, 'keeping such a delicious man to yourself!'

Serena remained silent, but Adam accepted the feminine flattery with a charming meaningless smile. 'How do you do, Miss Stamford?'

'Caroline, please,' the older girl pressed, letting her hand linger in his for longer than politeness dictated. 'Are you staying in Yorkshire?'

'For a while,' Adam answered her question but not the signals the brunette was sending.

'In that case, we must see you more often,' Caroline rebuked lightly, but there was something very purposeful in her rider of, 'That is, if young Serena can bear to share you around!'

'Steady on, Caro!' John protested mildly at the suggestive coupling of Serena and her cousin—as he thought of Adam.

'Darling Serena knows I was only teasing,' Caroline replied with a smile that was immediately cancelled out by the heavy condescension in the glance she gave Serena.

'I seldom take anything you say seriously, Caroline . . . darling,' Serena purred in a faultless imitation of the other girl's husky tone.

Unperturbed, Caroline curled one hand round John's arm with an easy familiarity and smiled engagingly at both men. 'What do you do for a living, Adam? Something terribly adventurous, I'll bet,' she simpered, managing to convey her approval of his hard-muscled physique by stopping just short of batting her black, unbelievably long eyelashes.

'I'm a writer of sorts,' Adam replied equably, inwardly amused by the he-man image he had just destroyed and turning his smile on the wrong girl.

'Oh, how fascinating!' Caroline exclaimed, obviously delighted at the possibility of claiming acquaintance with a celebrity. 'Under what name do you write?'

There was no mistaking the laughter Serena was struggling to control as Adam's gaze remained on her while replying blandly, 'My own.' He didn't resent the humour, only the fact that she rarely shared it with him.

'Oh, really?' For several seconds Caroline's extreme self-confidence slipped. 'My apologies, Adam, but I don't often get the time to read. Too busy on the farm, you understand.'

It was Adam's turn to stifle amusement at the incongruous vision of those scarlet-tipped fingers toiling on the land.

'You're a farmer too?' he returned with a creditable straight face, having once again caught Serena's eye.

'Yes, my father's and John's lands are adjoining.' Caroline supplied the information to Adam, but it was an almost forgotten John she looked up at, when she delivered an additional, 'Together they would make one of the biggest estates in the county.'

At this John went an unbecoming red, and Serena came to his rescue. 'It's getting late, John,' she reminded him softly, 'Perhaps we'd better be going.'

He was not given the chance to answer for himself before Caroline interceded, 'I hope you don't mind, sweetie, but John's offered me a lift back to my place with a horse that I bought on impulse at the farm auction.'

'Won't it be a squash in the Range Rover?' Adam quipped, growing to dislike the way Caroline Stamford talked to Serena, but the witticism was lost on the older girl, her good looks marred by a slightly vacant expression.

'Caro bought one of the horse boxes that was up for auction as well,' said John by way of explanation, and cast an apologetic look in Serena's direction. 'You don't mind, do you, making the detour?'

Adam recognised an opportunity and quickly took it. 'Serena can come back with me.'

'Well, if it's no trouble,' John mumbled reluctantly, caught between wanting to keep Serena with him but apart from his former girl-friend.

'Don't be silly, John—they're living in the same house, aren't they?' Caroline chipped in.

'Well, if you're sure you don't mind, Serena?' the younger man queried rather helplessly.

She shook her head, and Adam wondered if she could not trust herself to speak. If she refused to go with him, it would seem odd to John, and she seemed to strain at being very correct in front of him. But he wasn't taking any chances.

'Then if you're ready, Princess?'

'Why do you call her that?' Caroline's curiosity was roused, and along with it the memory of Serena and Adam Carmichael standing very close together just before John had pomped the horn.

'Just a pet name, isn't it, little one?' He circled Serena's small waist with his arm, as if to affirm the closeness of their relationship, gambling that she would not create a scene by wresting out of his grasp. He won his bet, but the heart that beat frantically above his fingers communicated her fury at his action.

'So sweet to see such affection between cousins, I loathe most of mine,' Caroline drawled. 'Don't you think so, John?'

Adam was wise to the game she was playing, but he doubted if the younger man was aware he was being manipulated into distrusting Serena.

'We're not really—cousins, I mean. Well, maybe of the kissing variety.' Adam replied, making the most of the situation.

'I thought we were leaving,' said Serena, barely civil in her tone.

Adam successfully foiled John's attempts at getting Serena on her own for a moment, as he escorted her to his car, and the second he had slammed his door he drove off, leaving a bemused John to Caroline Stamford's not-so-tender mercies.

Waiting for the eruption, he anticipated the bittersweet pleasure an argument would bring. Even in a rage, Serena was more captivating then any woman he had ever met. As though she sensed his expectancy, and was bent on cheating him, the first ten miles of the journey were accomplished in a tense silence which Adam eventually broke.

'John's a pretty willing fellow,' was his opening gambit.

And as if she had been waiting for it, Serena was ready, snapping back, 'For willing substitute weak, yes?'

'You're too quick for me, Princess,' Adam replied pleasantly. 'God knows how John keeps pace.'

'I don't . . .' she stopped mid-sentence.

'You don't what, Serena?' he pressed, flicking her a sideways glance.

'You're so damn clever, you tell me!'

Adam slowed the car before saying, 'I think you were about to say something to the effect that you don't reveal too much of your intelligence to John as you know he

couldn't cope.' She gave no indication whether she agreed
with him or not, but her silence was telling. 'Do you
believe you can be happily married to someone with
whom you can never really extend yourself for fear of
making him feel inferior?'

'So now we're an expert on marriage too,' she scoffed,
still staring rigidly ahead of her.

'No, I've just been around a little longer than you,'
Adam said patiently. 'Imagine what's going to happen
when you have a fight.'

'We don't fight.'

'How dull!'

'How ridiculous!' she mimicked.

They fell silent for several minutes and Adam knew she
had drifted away into her own thoughts. He wasn't sure if
he wanted to pursue the topic; the idea of Serena tying
herself to the young farmer he had met that afternoon
appalled him, but he had difficulty separating genuine
concern for her welfare from hard jealousy. He hadn't
been very successful earlier.

Her next question, almost devoid of animosity, surprised him. 'What did you mean—about having an argument?'

'Nothing, Princess. Just my own bitterness spilling out.'

'I want to hear it,' she insisted.

Adam tried to read what was going through the pretty
little head turned towards him, but he couldn't concentrate on driving and Serena at one and the same time.
There was no contest; he slowed down and pulled into the
next layby.

Switching off the engine, he moved slowly round in his
seat. He still had her full attention and he wondered if he
had gained it by voicing doubts she had already formed.

He strived for an impersonal note that wouldn't offend
as he explained, 'I would say you are much brighter than
John and that's going to show every time you argue about
anything—inevitable in the best of marriages, and with-

out our own problem in getting along, I think you have a fair amount of rage inside you.' She looked on the verge of hot denial so he continued quietly, 'It comes out in your paintings, Princess. Either you learn to turn the other cheek or you end up putting the other person down. Do you think John could live with that?'

'Why the sudden concern for John?' she countered suspiciously.

'It's not. It's for you, little one,' Adam replied, softness in his eyes and voice. 'One of the most common responses when a man finds himself up against a woman a lot smarter than he, more articulate, is one of physical violence. A primitive but effective way of re-establishing male dominance.'

'You're talking rot,' she protested indignantly, 'with regard to John anyway.'

'Maybe, but sometimes, Princess, when I'm very near to slapping you instead I try to get my revenge verbally. What's John going to do when you dig your sharp little claws into him and draw blood?' he reminded her how hard she could push when she was in a temper.

Her eyes were swiftly lowered, and she mumbled, 'It's not like that with John.'

Leaning forward, Adam cupped her chin in his hand till her eyes, shadowed with uncertainty, were level with his once more, and asked quietly, 'What's it like, Serena?'

'It's . . . It's . . .' she searched for a word to fit her relationship with John and the disturbance Adam's steady scrutiny was causing, gave it to her. 'It's peaceful.'

'Peaceful!' Adam repeated incredulously, scornfully. 'You enjoy driving a man to hell and back, Serena Templeton, and you tell me you want peace!'

'Yes. Yes, I do,' she declared. 'He makes me feel norm . . . ordinary.'

It slipped out in the rise of her ready temper but was left hanging in the sudden hush that followed, Serena looking confused and shamed by her admission while Adam was moved to pity by it.

'Oh, Princess,' he groaned, one hand gentle on the curve of her shoulder, 'you'll never be ordinary. You're fire and ice, special and gifted, and trying to hide it is just plain madness.'

It was the word 'madness' that must have done it, Adam later concluded—that sent her shying away from his sympathy and clambering out of his car before he realised his unfortunate choice of words. His physical reactions were quicker, and he caught up with her before she was ten yards down the road.

'Where in God's name do you think you're going?' He sounded harsh from the shock her sudden flight had given him, not improved by her apparent coolness as she continued walking at a steady pace. 'Come back to the car!'

'Home.' She didn't break her stride, didn't even turn her head when she muttered tightly, 'Mad people can be a liability in moving vehicles.'

It broke Adam's resolve not to be rough on her, as he pulled her to a sharp halt, and when she tried to twist from his grip, clamped his hand hard down on her waist.

'Now listen, and listen good! With both ears and all that brain power you intend to waste on your simple farming boy.' He dragged her closer till their faces were bare inches apart, and she looked startled by the anger vibrating his voice.

'I'm sick of having everything I say misinterpreted so that it fits my villainous personality, and I am not going to spend the rest of our lives bending over backwards not to offend your sensibilities while you cut me up with your vicious little tongue. I'm only human, girl, not some cold-blooded creature or a martyred saint, and I'd have to be one or other to take it. Do you understand?' Adam demanded.

Serena understood, enough to be choked by the pain threading his accusation, much more real than any imagined hurt she had made as an excuse to run out on their discussion.

The tears came trickling down from the enormous eyes staring up at him, and although she hadn't realised she was crying till the first drop reached her trembling lips, Serena did not try to hide it. The tears were a gift to him—a little girl saying she was sorry for being bad, but Adam had never wanted it, couldn't take it. He drew her towards him and buried her face in the curve of his shoulder so he wouldn't have to see the distress he had wrought in temper and frustration. Even the quiet sobbing muffled by his jacket had a stranglehold over his heart that made it difficult to breathe, and yet part of him wanted to hold her there for ever.

But Serena needed to say something once the tears had passed. Withdrawing from his arms, she started to wipe her eyes with the back of her hand and mumbled a shy, 'Thanks,' when he offered her his handkerchief. She scrubbed her face dry and raised her head determinedly, only to have every thought in it, chased away by the expression on his face—full of tenderness and concern for her. She seemed to see him for the first time without the past blurring her vision and wasn't conscious of her fixed stare until he spoke.

'Have I grown two heads since I shaved this morning?' Adam teased, and as a test to see if her steady appraisal had worked in his favour, it was completely successful. Serena smiled, slow and shy, the most beautiful smile he had ever seen. He had to know, but he kept it light, 'Still hate me?'

Serena shook her head, but her face straightened into seriousness. If she didn't keep the courage to tell him now, they might never get to this point again.

'She lied to me, said you'd have me locked away. And afterwards, when you came back, I got you mixed up with her . . .' She wasn't being too clear now either, but he came to her rescue as she faltered.

'It's OK, Princess, I understand.' Adam didn't want to put her through an exorcism any more, not at the risk of losing the precious ground he appeared to have gained. He placed a tentative arm round her shoulders. 'Let's go home.'

She hesitated for a second and he gave her a light brotherly hug before leading her back to the Porsche and installing her in the passenger seat. By the time he had gone round to the other side and climbed in, the girl next to him looked very far away.

He touched a cold hand lying on her lap. 'Fasten your seatbelt, Princess.'

It returned her to him, and he wasn't ready for her question. 'Why don't you want to know about Andrea any more?' His silence was received with disappointment and she muttered quickly, 'It doesn't matter.'

'You don't give people much of a chance, Serena,' Adam scolded mildly. 'Are you sure you want to talk about it?' She was sitting tense as a coiled spring but nodded. 'Last week I paid a visit to Simon Clarke and he supplied me with the details you'd given him about Andrea's behaviour towards you.'

'Those lies!' Serena interrupted brokenly. 'I bet you found them amusing. Your dear refined aunt the child abuser—ridiculous, isn't it?'

'Is it?' Adam murmured softly, as all the old defiance came back into the eyes holding his. He was being tested and expected to fail. Her trust didn't come easily either. 'She was sad and sick. And maybe her reasons for harming you could be termed ridiculous. But none of the bare facts you threw at Clarke were designed to raise laughter.'

'You *believed* them.' It came out as a whisper but was a shout of wonder inside Serena's head.

'They were the truth,' said Adam with conviction, and then almost casually, 'Why should't I?'

'Simon didn't. He called them implausible . . .' She flushed guiltily.

'You read his report?' Adam astutely guessed.

'He left it lying around,' Serena defended halfhearted-ly, 'and it was about me.'

Adam neatly laughed, but confined himself to an amused, 'Poor Clarke, it's small wonder that he didn't abandon his profession after being led around in circles by his patient, expected to swallow whole and in the space of five minutes what he'd been trying to discover for twelve months, and then ostracised for not immediately doing so!'

He was gambling by making light of the sensitive subject, believing it needed fresh air.

It coaxed a half-smile from her lips before she pouted, 'He was silly and sometimes too obvious for words.'

'Well, if it's any consolation, he would like to come and apologise for the mistake he made.'

'No.' It was very decisive, and when Adam's eyebrows lifted in enquiry, Serena added regretfully, 'I was mean to him and perhaps I didn't give him much of a chance to help, but I don't want to see him again . . . please!'

Her eyelashes were now lowered as a shield, but Adam detected the fact that she was rather ashamed of her behaviour to the young psychiatrist, but more worrying, she was humiliated by ever needing him.

'You don't have to,' Adam affirmed quickly. 'I'll write him a letter if you like.'

'If you would, I'd be . . . grateful.'

It was his mother's sweet little girl talking, but natural, not forced. It stirred his conscience. 'We'd better be moving before my mother thinks we're both deserting her for dinner tonight.'

'I've been childish, haven't I?' Serena admitted solemnly, and Adam wondered if he would ever stop being surprised by the things she said.

Adam smiled down at her. '*You're* twenty years old, Princess. What's my excuse?'

She actually thought about it, before matching his

levity as she suggested, 'Provocation?' then laughed at his momentary disconcertment, her eyes gleaming with mischief a provocation in themselves.

She has no idea of her power, Adam thought, as he joined her laughter, although he was sorely tempted to lean towards her enchanting mouth and do something that would be utter stupidity in the present circumstances. Her trust was as fragile and precious as fine porcelain.

He turned his concentration to getting them home and in other people's company as quickly as possible, while Serena looked out of her window, her expression moving with her thoughts between a frown and a smile.

When they drew up at the front door Adam asked simply, 'Am I in to dinner?' and held his breath for the answer.

It was slow in coming and indirect, setting the pattern for their relationship in the near future.

'I'll go and tell Mrs Baker,' Serena offered courteously before scrambling out of the car with more haste than dignity to do just that.

Adam watched her retreating back till she disappeared into the house, and silently committed himself to do no more than that from then on. To watch and wait, and above all put her happiness before anything else.

CHAPTER NINE

Two months ago it had started with Serena accepting Adam's invitations as penance for the gross misjudgment she had made of his character.

They went riding together, and, apart from helping her on and off her horse, he never touched her. He took her round every notable gallery in London, a veritable marathon, and proved himself capable of giving her an education in art history more enjoyable than any provided in dull textbooks, for it was laced with his wry humour; and on the way home, when she had almost spoilt a perfect day with a snide comment about not needing a substitute father, he had sensed and redressed the imbalance she was feeling with a confounding offer for her to criticise the first chapters of his latest novel.

Serena had felt too shy to take him up on it, but he had dumped the manuscript in her lap after dinner one evening. The next night he had listened and encouraged while she tried to give an unbiased opinion, impossible when she was so nervous of displeasing him now, and had laughed goodnaturedly when she had commented that it lacked the biting edge that made his characters nasty but interesting.

He had taken her out to dinner and a few times to the theatre in Leeds, but those invitations always included Nancy. And all three had spent a weekend in London; it had been enjoyable, apart from the Saturday afternoon when the two women went shopping, and Serena felt guilty because her enthusiasm was forced and had failed to channel her mind from wondering where Adam had disappeared after dropping them in the Old Brompton Road. He had made up for it in the evening by taking them to a play written by the friend with whom he had spent the afternoon.

She was neglecting John, avoiding dinner dates and once actually forgetting one when Adam had arrived home unexpectedly early from a business trip to London. It had been embarrassing: John at the door in his best suit and Serena standing open-mouthed in jeans and paint-smeared top, and the Carmichaels left to entertain him while she changed in record time. And the sight of Adam playing host with impeccable politeness had convinced her that any sexual interest she had aroused in him had been killed by the knowledge of how his aunt had treated her. What had seemed like jealousy of John had simply been his way of showing her what she now knew to be fact—marriage to John Saxon would be a disastrous mistake, for both of them.

From the day of the auction she had understood what Adam was trying to do—in some way compensate for his aunt's ill-treatment, by being guardian, friend, confidant, whatever she wanted him to be. There was no pressure to do so, but she gave him some of her bad memories and he helped to reduce their significance by making her see Andrea as pathetic rather than demonic, to be pitied for a jealously so extreme that she had taken it out on a child who had looked too like her mother and was loved too much by her father.

But she had let a new fear take the place of the others—that one day she would rise early, throw on her riding clothes and run down the stairs to find White Lightning without a master, the Porsche no longer in the garage and Adam a thousand miles away. It was what she had to expect; Nancy had told her long ago that he rarely remained in England for a whole summer—often stayed months on end in a country that captured his interest.

It was a silly fear in one sense, for the man she now knew wouldn't leave without saying goodbye—but very soon he wouldn't be her guardian.

He would have fulfilled the obligation he had admitted to feeling when she had asked why he had come to Yorkshire, and he would be free. And there was very little she could do to keep him here.

Suddenly it was the end of term at college, and the prospect that by the end of the summer Adam would have gone filled her with a quiet despair.

She had cleared her locker and, arms laden down with books and portfolios, was walking out into the sunshine with the other girls catching the bus to the station when she stopped short. The Porsche sat outside the main gates with Adam casually leaning against the bonnet.

'Wow, what a fabulous car!' one of the girls exclaimed.

'What a fabulous man, you mean,' said another. 'I'd like him for my birthday—and without gift wrapping, if you get my drift.'

'Whose is he anyway?' asked a third.

'He's my cousin,' said Serena before any further comments were made, and betrayed herself with a blush to the roots of her hair, before bidding the others a hasty farewell.

'Tell that to the Marines!' Cathy called after her as she almost ran to intercept Adam, and it started the others giggling, which made Serena feel unreasonably cross with him for being what he was, a handsome and very attractive male.

Little of her original elation on seeing him remained when she reached him, and although he emptied her arms and muttered something about end-of-term clutter, he looked none too pleased either.

The impression was reinforced as he stowed her gear in the boot with a slam and impatiently clicked on his seatbelt. It annoyed her into announcing ungraciously, 'You didn't have to come, you know. I could have taken the train.'

'I wanted to,' he replied, his grim face implying something else.

'It sounds like it,' Serena said sulkily, and instantly regretted it. All day worrying about him leaving before she stopped needing him around, and now she was behaving in a manner that might guarantee it!

'I'm sorry. Thanks for coming, Adam.' It solicited a smile that made the sun come out again for Serena.

'My fault,' Adam muttered self-deprecatingly. 'I don't like being giggled over, especially when I can guess the reason.'

'I didn't like it either,' Serena hastily set the record straight. 'And what do you imagine they were saying?'

He refused to meet her eyes but answered moodily, 'Who's your dad, or words to that effect.'

It set Serena off, but she couldn't help it. 'It's absurd, Cathy thinks . . .' she managed, before the rest was swallowed up by laughter.

Adam's tone was sobering, as he struggled to keep his temper. 'What does Cathy think?'

'She thinks,' Serena expanded, trying to keep her face straight, 'that she'd like you as a birthday present, but she'd dispense with the gift-wrapping. And believe me, that was very euphemistic for Cathy!' She'd expected it would make him look a little less forbidding, but if anything it made it worse. 'She meant that . . .'

'I know what she meant,' he interrupted brusquely.

Serena wasn't too sure how she had caused offence, but the black look he was giving her started her nervously biting her lip.

The transformation in Adam was immediate and total as his hand came up to stroke the hair from her face and he said softly, 'I'm not mad with you, Princess. And you're right, I am being absurd. What you think is all that matters.'

If there was the merest hint of question in his quiet statement, she wasn't given the time to form an answer before he lightly touched her cheek and then leaned back to switch on the engine. It was just as well, because when he looked at her like that, his eyes lazy with indulgence and the beginnings of a smile on his firm lips, feeling took over from thought, and she didn't want to embarrass him with it—even if she could have articulated her chaotic emotions.

The day was very warm and Adam pulled open the sun-roof when they were away from the city fumes. A pleasant breeze filled the car and the conversation was aimless and pleasant, just right for a summer day. They arrived home much sooner than Serena would have liked.

Adam dropped her at the door and she went in search of Nancy, reflecting on the ways her relationship with the older woman had altered too. It was more equal, less adult and child, and consequently more satisfying for them both. The two women nearly collided on the threshold of the lounge.

'You're early.' Nancy's shock at finding Serena home made her slow to react, and Serena was breezing into the lounge with a cheerful, 'Yes, Adam came to collect me. I had mountains of rubbish and he . . .'

When she realised Nancy was not alone, Serena's natural reticence reasserted itself and she tailed off mid-sentence. Later she was to wonder how she guessed the stranger's identity before she even spoke.

The redhead rose languidly, her slanting eyes quickly assessing and mentally dismissing, and Nancy broke in hurriedly, 'Serena, this is a—friend of Adam's, Julia Hamlisch.'

Julia laughed throatily at the hesitant introduction and, every inch the sophisticate in sleeveless white satin, strolled forward and drawled with a pointedly slow diction, 'You must be Adam's little cousin. How are you, dear?'

The woman was talking to her as if she was an idiot, and for a long second all Serena could do was gape, confirming it.

'Where's Adam?' Nancy urged at her elbow.

It snapped Serena out of her daze sufficiently to answer, 'The garage.'

The only one equal to the situation was Julia, too insensitive to feel any awkwardness, as she took a bemused Serena's arm. 'Come and sit with me on the sofa, dear, while Nancy breaks the news of my arrival to Adam. Men can be so funny about surprises we women spring on them!'

It was probably the only thing that could have made Nancy leave Serena in the same room with Julia—the need to warn Adam. For as unpredictable as her son could be, the last few months made it certain that his reaction would be far from favourable to Julia's return.

'And has Adam been taking you for a little jaunt in his car, dear?' Julia continued in the same painful tone when Nancy had scurried out of the lounge.

It made Serena shrink instinctively away from the woman's cloying sweetness and brought her back to full awareness. 'I think you've made a mistake,' she declared with an incisive clarity. 'I have all my faculties, mental and physical. I can read, write and count backwards from a hundred on a good day.' She was being shockingly rude, and she didn't care. The hurt was unbearable, for there was only one person from whom this dreadful woman could have gained the belief that she was a simpleton.

'So I hear,' Julia eventually managed, and stared hard and calculatingly at the sharp-eyed opponent confronting her. The girl's features seemed more than a little familiar, but she could not place why. 'Adam was so touchy whenever I mentioned you, I assumed . . .' she left it hanging in mid-air as she connected Serena with a certain portrait, and murmured speculatively, 'I obviously misread the situation.'

But Serena no longer cared what Julia thought as the pendulum swung back in Adam's favour at the word touchy, and when he literally burst into the room, part of her heart went out to him as his eyes, protective and caring, sought her out first. Within seconds it was crushed.

Before Adam could fend her off, Julia threw her arms up and kissed him on the lips. Roughly he tore her hands from his neck and pushed her away.

'Darling, you're not still mad with me, are you?' Julia purred seductively, and damned him by glibly lying, 'And I've come back to England just as you wanted!'

'Excuse me,' Serena mumbled, embarrassed at witnessing Julia's passionate embrace and tears already moistening her eyelashes. She didn't see the arms outstretched to her as she hurried out of the room.

Julia's shrill laughter stopped Adam from following. 'Emotional little thing—the mad cousin. Quite pretty in a washed-out sort of way.' It was said to evoke a response, and Julia got more than she bargained for as Adam wheeled round, eyes blazing.

'You've got exactly five minutes to tell me what you're doing here,' he gritted out.

'That's not very welcoming, Adam darling,' she pouted with false sweetness. 'Gerry told me you were staying up here and I thought . . . well, absence makes the heart grow fonder, and all that.'

She really was unbelievable. 'Where's Melvin?' Julia arched her pencil-thin eyebrows, and he added derisively, 'The fat rich producer you married.'

'Oh—that Melvin. Getting fatter and richer in London,' she laughed wickedly, 'while I visit my sick mother in Yorkshire.'

Adam didn't flatter himself. Julia was bored, and looking for excitement any way she could get it.

'Well, your sick mother has just recovered,' he stated flatly, 'and she's about to drive you down to the station. Where are your bags?'

'How cruel! And after I've come all the way up to this dreary place to let bygones be bygones,' Julia simpered, lips pouting, and resumed her seat to reach for her cigarettes. 'I would have thought you'd welcome some entertainment, darling.'

'Julia, I don't seem to be making myself clear. You're leaving. Tonight. Now!' he stressed the last. 'I don't need any entertainment, at least none that you could provide.'

At last Julia understood that Adam meant to reject her, although the message had needed to penetrate several layers of vanity.

'Oh, I get it,' she sneered, carelessly flicking ash on the carpet. 'The sweet young thing.'

'Julia!' he warned.

'Cradle-snatching. Still, you're the right age for it,' she said bitterly, her catlike eyes narrowing. 'But I can't see that skinny body amusing you in bed for long.'

He should have been used to her bitchiness, but when applied to Serena he found it intolerable. 'Just shut up!' he shouted angrily, giving credence to pure speculation. 'Leave Serena out of this!'

'How touching! Does the object of your love return it, I wonder?' She smiled mockingly at him, knowing that his mother being in the house gave her immunity against the storm brewing in his dark eyes.

Adam cursed himself for giving her a stick with which to beat him, but he would not deny his love as though he was ashamed of it.

'What have you been saying to her?' he demanded threateningly.

'Nothing that wasn't fit for the delicate infant's ears.' Julia was enjoying sniping at Serena, for Adam's obvious preference more than rankled. It brought back memories, conveniently forgotten when she had became bored with London and Melvin, of his indifference in America and before. 'Although I must say she did seem rather piqued that I believed her to be ga-ga.'

Julia's soft insidious remark unintentionally transformed Adam's rising fury to a mute despair at a vision of Serena, wild and hurting at the misconception he had never corrected. He lost total interest in Julia, crossing to the drinks cabinet and pouring himself a stiff drink. He downed it in one swallow.

Julia was not so easily dismissed; she arrived at his side when he was refilling his glass, with a caustic, 'Still drinking, I see.'

It revived his lost year in Hollywood, and killed the taste for another drink. 'I'll drive you back to Leeds,' he muttered coolly, shrugging off the hand that had appeared on his sleeve.

'Like an unwanted piece of baggage. I wonder what the child will think of such uncivilised behaviour.' Julia's face was alive with malice. 'It's almost as though you were afraid to have me in the house.'

Adam immediately saw her implication: if he showed himself so anxious to be rid of Julia, it might suggest he nurtured some feeling for his ex-girl-friend. The only emotion he felt was a hard contempt, but would others see it that way?—and Julia was determined to have the situation such that she did not lose face.

He compromised. 'You can stay one night, but you leave first thing in the morning.'

'I thought you might see it my way, darling,' she mocked his weakness with a twisted smile. 'Mustn't give the impression that you still want me to . . . anyone.'

'Dinner's at eight,' he replied with heavy restraint. It was going to be a long evening and for once he hoped that Serena had made arrangements to go out with John Saxon.

'I must go and change, darling.' Julia's mind was already ticking over on how to put the competition well back in the shade. 'Your mother's already shown me my room.'

No doubt his mother had been backed into a corner by Julia's unrepentant nerve. With incredulity he finally asked, 'You didn't really believe I'd welcome you back?'

'Not on a permanent basis,' Julia admitted freely, but

continued, as she closed the gap between them, 'But in one department we used to get along quite well.'

'My memory doesn't stretch that far back,' Adam responded cuttingly, after setting her firmly at arm's length. He had never loved her and now found it inconceivable that he had once found her attractive.

'We'll see,' Julia declared with a soft menace, before swaying out of the room.

He was left in no doubt that her innuendoes meant trouble and prayed that his mother was upstairs right at this minute, following his instruction to persuade Serena to go out for dinner. He had caught the anguish when he had entered the room and seen the tears held back while she ran to the door—and Julia had only been alone with her for minutes!

Nancy Carmichael was fervently praying for the end of the meal. Nervously her attention shifted between the other occupants of the room as if she was in the presence of a time bomb that threatened explosion at any moment.

The contrast between the two women in her son's life was striking. Julia was dressed in a chic off-the-shoulder gown, singularly inappropriate for the occasion. While Serena, surprisingly adamant about her intention to dine in, appeared to have selected her wardrobe with the express purpose of being as nondescript as possible—her lack of sophistication emphasised by a simple blouse topping slightly worn red velvet trousers and her hair bound tightly into a long braid.

After several unsuccessful attempts to catch her eye, Adam had adopted a cool impersonal mask and, for the most part, concentrated on pointedly ignoring Julia's efforts to engage him in conversation. Nancy was left to act as reluctant hostess, and by the dessert, it almost seemed the meal could be completed without any major outburst of the tension that electrified the atmosphere.

'How old are you anyway, sweetie?' Julia asked suddenly, addressing the younger woman for the first time since the meal began.

Serena looked up, startled by her abrupt inclusion in the conversation. 'Twenty-one next birthday,' she offered reluctantly.

'You look somehow . . . *younger*. Doesn't she, Adam darling?' And without giving him the opportunity to comment, she pressed on, 'And have you a job? So many girls do these days.' She made it sound like a practice to be despised.

'I'm at college,' Serena managed to reply, before . . .

'Oh, how clever! And what are you studying? No, don't tell me. Let me guess.' Julia made a show of reflection, her narrowed appraisal successfully stripping the girl opposite to the bone. 'I know—domestic science. So useful—an asset many men consider almost as important as beauty— or at least as a compensation for its absence.' Despite being fundamentally a stupid woman, Julia had spent a lifetime perfecting her ability to incisively undermine any female who got in her way. In such a few ostensibly polite remarks, she had conveyed the impression that Serena was both plain and stupid.

'Really, Julia, must you badger my . . . ward?' Adam struggled, reaching for a means to divert the direction of the conversation.

'Ward?' Julia's laughter, brittle and derisive, registered suspended disbelief. 'Well, that's a new word for it, darling!'

Nancy, on the verge of challenging Julia's insinuation, was discouraged by the slight shake of Adam's head in silent warning. Instead it was Serena who took it up as Adam had been scared she would; meekness was not one of her character traits.

'What does that mean, Mrs Hamlisch? I'm afraid I'm not familiar with the subtleties of sophisticated *small* talk.' It should have been a very definite discouragement, but for the fact that the implied insult washed completely over Julia's insensitive head.

'Oh, honey pie, you're such an innocent,' Julia drawled with shades of a transatlantic twang. 'Still, with Adam's expert coaching that should be soon rectified.'

'I suppose it was too much to expect you to behave in a civilised manner for a whole evening,' Adam said icily, losing hope of avoiding a scene.

'Coming from you, that's rich, darling. I wonder if the dear child has had the dubious pleasure of your company when you're on one of your alcoholic binges. Perhaps we should compare notes, as ex and current mistresses . . .' Julia left it hanging, satisfied that he would be jolted out of his infuriating indifference.

She got her wish as the wine glass she had been toying with was sent flying from her hand and she gaped open-mouthed at the hand lifting to strike. The action was inhibited, not by his mother's horrified protest, but by catching the expression of hurt that Serena wore as she desperately pushed out of her chair and ran to the door.

Adam was torn between the need to throw Julia bodily out of the house and the desire to follow Serena. The decision was taken out of his hands.

'I'm scared. Go after her, Adam,' his mother exhorted anxiously.

Deaf to Julia's disgusted mutter of 'Such a baby!' he ran up the staircase. Assuming he would find Serena weeping on her bed, he was chilled by the emptiness of the room. Intuitively he went to the window and peered out into the night. Within seconds he was reacting to the light that flickered in the darkness and taking the shortest route to the studio by the scullery door.

She stood at the old wooden table, ripping up sketches with a desperation that scattered the pieces to the floor.

'For God's sake, stop it, Princess!' he snapped, confusing command and appeal in his tone. Wresting the remaining drawings from her frantic grasp, he dropped them back on the table—and was thrown momentarily off balance by the picture of his own distinctive features staring up at him.

Serena's tear-streaked face blazed anger and without fear she wildly attacked him, her fists raining blows on his broad chest. 'I hate you! I hate you, Adam Carmichael!' she screamed up at him.

Catching her wrists, more to stop her hurting herself than because of any pain she was managing to inflict, Adam merely succeeded in transferring her method of assault. Using her feet as weapons, she unrestrainedly kicked out with painful accuracy. Grabbing her by the waist, Adam swung her off her feet and into his arms: keeping her off balance seemed the only way of blunting her attack.

'Put me down!' she commanded, mustering as much dignity as was possible in the circumstances, but squirming so much she was likely to topple them both over.

He carried her over to a threadbare armchair in a corner of the studio and carefully eased them both down, frustrating her immediate struggle to get free.

'Calm down,' he soothed, as she suddenly went rigid. 'I'm not going to hurt you.'

Her ironic laughter had more than an element of hysteria and was quickly replaced by gulping sobs when she abruptly gave up any resistance and collapsed into his arms. He gathered her closer until her head was curled under his chin and held her tightly while her tears soaked his shirt. That she sought his comfort brought a strange joy that warred with the guilt of having caused her misery. He wanted to cry, and laugh, too, but stayed very quiet and still, waiting for her crying to subside.

Serena blew her nose in his handkerchief and bit back more tears as he gently rocked her.

'Still hate me?' he whispered softly against her forehead.

Very slowly she moved her head from side to side against his chest, but when she tried her voice, it sounded low and fierce. 'I hate *her*, though!'

It was an emotion Adam wholeheartedly shared at that precise moment, but his own anger was secondary to the need to explain the scene at dinner.

'Listen, Princess—as you probably know, Julia was once my mistress. We didn't part on particularly good terms and unfortunately she's chosen you as a way to get back at me. But it's nothing personal to you—a wild, crazy accusation even she doesn't believe.'

Her reply was totally unanticipated as she lifted her head. 'You're like her—you think I'm too young and stupid to know what's going on,' she muttered, anger beneath the unhappiness, and he did not try to detain her when she wriggled out of his arms and moved away from him.

With quick, jerky movements she started to clear the mess she had made and replaced the ripped and crumpled drawings back on the table, then just as suddenly stopped what she was doing to grip hard on to the edge. She did not turn as Adam approached, but neither did she shrug off the hands that he laid gently on her shoulders.

'She wanted to make me look gauche and childish in your eyes,' Serena mumbled dejectedly, staring down at the torn sketches, 'and she succeeded.'

'Oh, little one . . .' Adam groaned. It was the worst endearment he could have used in the circumstances.

'Stop treating me like a child!' Her back went ramrod stiff under his fingers. 'She wants you back, doesn't she? For you to go away with her?'

Adam obeyed her request in his frankness. 'No, she's married now to a Hollywood producer, and knowing her husband, the happy event was preceded by a trip to his lawyers to ensure she doesn't get a penny in the event of a divorce. She knows she wouldn't get the financial security of a marriage certificate from me.'

She had half turned to read his expression and, frowning, asked, 'Then why has she come to see you?'

'Who knows?' Adam sighed. He didn't want to go into his past with Serena, but his evasion was met with a sharp, 'Are you still in love with her?' and when he failed to answer straight away, was followed with an embarrassed, 'I'm sorry, I have no right to ask. It's none of my business.'

'You're still not giving people a chance, Princess,' he chided mildly, trailing a finger over the worried crease of her brow. 'I'm not still in love with her, because I never was. As you've noticed, she's not a very lovable person.'

'You lived with her,' Serena stated quizzically.

Again Adam was confronted with the black and white certainty of youth, but this time he did not duck the issue.

'Julia is a beautiful woman whom I met at a party about three years ago. We had an adult affair based on mutual benefit without the complication of love. It was already entering its death throes before I went to America, but she followed me there because she'd come to the end of her first divorce settlement.' Serena was absorbing it all, but what she was making of his dry words, it was impossible to tell. Adam read her next question, however, and preempted it with, 'At that period my self-respect was at an all-time low. I was on my way down and I didn't really care enough to shake off Julia.'

Serena continued to look steadily up at him and he wondered if she was searching for other signs of weakness when she declared very seriously, 'But you're on your way up now, aren't you, Adam?'

Sometimes he didn't understand where her questions were leading, hadn't quite figured out the half child, half woman that was Serena Templeton, but a glimmer of hope had been born over the last few weeks.

'Yes, I suppose I am.' His smile wasn't returned, but

she seemed more contemplative than annoyed as she averted her attention to piecing together two halves of the uppermost sketch. He aimed for casualness.

'Do I really look that grim?'

'Mm, sometimes when you don't realise anyone is watching you,' she murmured.

'And then?'

She sorted through the sketches and selected another along with the comment, 'Confident. Self-assured.'

'Image preservation,' he said wryly, thinking of how insecure he was about the girl standing beside him. 'And when I'm looking at you, Princess?—This one?' He pointed at the only portrait with him smiling, his eyes lightened with his feelings for the artist. Serena nodded. Strange that she could capture his emotion on paper and yet not be able to interpret it. 'You're very talented, you know. One day the rich and famous will be lining up to be immortalised by your skill. Perhaps I should pay you a fee if you're going to do my portrait.'

'Don't be silly,' she said crossly, not sure if he was teasing and obviously shy about the sketches she had already done in secret.

Her sharpness did not bother Adam; he was used to the reprimand. Sometimes it even made him smile. 'Perhaps I could give you another in exchange.'

'A painting?' she frowned up at him.

'Yes.' Adam, hoping he had chosen the right moment, went on, smilingly, 'I bought rather a good one at an auction a while back—mother and child.'

'But you paid so much!' she exclaimed astoundedly.

'I bought it for you then—as a goodbye present—but now . . .' he pulled a wry face—the possibility of his leaving while she was still there was inconceivable to Adam. Brushing the back of his hand against her cheek, he said quietly, 'It was to remind you of your childhood in Italy. The golden days, you've called them, with your mother and father. It should be yours.'

But Serena wasn't listening, hadn't really heard anything after his 'goodbye present'.

'Do you want to . . .' she hesitated, but when Adam smiled down at her, she swallowed hard and forced herself to continue, 'Would you like to sleep with me?'

Her blunt question, low and flat, struck him like a physical blow and brought back a suppressed memory of her taunting him with experience he had discarded as makebelieve. A cold, relentless fury crept over him as he caught her by the arm, fingers biting into flesh. 'Is that how you repay kindness from a man, or do you think I have to buy a woman in order to get her into my bed?' he demanded hoarsely. Wanting this girl to cherish for the rest of his life, he was shattered by the casual offer of a transitory sexual relationship.

'No, that's not . . .' The rest stuck in her throat, blocked there by Adam's dark, murderous expression.

'Are you suggesting we confirm Julia's sordid suspicions?' he pursued raggedly, 'or is this some cruel little test?'

'You're twisting things,' she cried in protest, trying to pull free from his bruising grip. 'I thought . . .'

He cut into her explanation. 'You thought I go around seducing little girls for the hell of it!' he shouted angrily, beyond reason. 'Nothing's changed, has it? Perhaps I'd better live up to my reputation!'

It was meant as a punishment, an assuagement for the hurt she could so easily inflict, but the sweet taste of her mouth dissolved all the rancour, leaving in its wake the heady, weakening sensation of wanting her with every fibre of his being. He lifted his lips from hers and for a second studied her perfection. Her lips were bruised and trembling, her eyes soft with invitation. He took it, and uninhibitedly her mouth began to answer his arousal with a fierce passion of its own, as naturally as though they had made love a thousand times. He felt the top buttons of her blouse give to his exploring hand and needed to push further, to lay his palm against the swell of her breast. A low moan escaped her throat as his fingers spread inside her lacy underwear and reached the tip of her breast, already pulsating with life. As she pressed her slight frame closer, it seemed that every part of him was riotously alive to her touch; this girl needed no lessons on how to turn a man on. And yet his spirit rebelled even while his body hardened with longing for her, and he jerked her back from him.

Her look of frustrated disbelief was crippling. Her breathing, shallow and spasmodic, almost made him forget pride and conscience.

'I don't understand.' It was the plea of a confused child at some inexplicable injustice of the adult world, and conditioned Adam's response.

'Simple. I don't make love to children, and I have no desire to act as stand-in for John while you improve your technique,' he announced harshly, at that moment despising himself for the weakness he had for her, knew he would always have. To him, her lovemaking spoke of a new sexual awareness that had not been present in their first kiss; he tortured himself with the image of her responding to another man's passion. 'Go to bed! Now!'

Horrified, Serena backed away from him, eyes wide and accusing.

'For a clever man, you can be incredibly stupid!' she cried before she turned and ran.

Without knowing the reasoning behind her parting shot, Adam fully agreed with her. Experience, not arrogance, told him she would have lain with him, there, on the studio floor, let him love her completely. He ached for her and realised that he had since his first day back—and yet he knew that to possess her only once would be infinitely worse.

It was poetic justice that would surely have been appreciated by some of the women who had called him bastard for cutting loose from anything taking the shape of heavy involvement. He wanted Serena Templeton, but tied to him for her life, not free to come and go to another man, and settling for less, a small part given out of gratitude or curiosity or whatever unfathomable emotion had been ruling her head at the time, he wasn't quite ready to contemplate. Tomorrow he'd get rid of Julia. And perhaps inch by inch in the coming summer he would make up the ground he had lost tonight.

CHAPTER TEN

By eight the next morning Adam was driving towards Leeds with an unusually taciturn Julia. Her silence he assumed was not due to any contrition for her conduct but a rare show of common sense that made her hold her vicious tongue.

She had said enough already. Apparently her love of drama had not been satisfied by the scene she had created at dinner. When he had returned from walking off his frustration she had been waiting for him. As she languidly uncurled herself from his bedroom armchair in sheer nylon that barely covered her full breasts the message had been clear.

She had underlined it with, 'I met the sweet young thing while she was making another *mad* dash for the stairs. But she stopped just long enough to say "He's all yours". Well, darling, I took her at her word.'

Hard incredulity had changed to cold contempt, and Adam had used the sort of language a woman like Julia would understand.

She had dropped the seductive quality from her voice, taunting, 'Why, I do believe you really love the girl!' She had found that amusing, laughing maliciously, 'And maybe she hasn't got all her marbles—but even she has the sense to realise that you and she . . . well, lover, it's on the sick side of ridiculous!'

He hadn't intended to give her the chance to say more, and something in his expression must have told her to back rapidly to the door—but she had left her poison in his system.

He had been bedding Julia and her like for more years than he cared to remember—the sort of woman you could walk away from without any crisis of conscience. It had made him a proficient lover, nothing more.

But he had outgrown that past, hadn't he? He had done nothing to hurt Serena, had treated her almost as a sister until he ached with the effort it cost. He made her laugh, was there when she needed to talk and allowed her to expend some of that inner anger against him although he had not caused it. Her sweet apologies made it worthwhile. Loving the girl had made him a different man from the Adam Carmichael those other women had known, hadn't it?

It was with relief that he eventually turned into the station square, carelessly leaving his car on a prohibited area in his haste to be rid of Julia. Luck was with him, for the London train was already standing on the platform.

His basic good manners forced him to carry her luggage to a first class carriage, but it was only her sharp taunting remark that delayed his departure.

'Well, good luck with your young playmate. Something tells me you'll need it, after our little assignation!'

'Nothing happened between us,' he growled down at her.

'Well, darling, you and I know that, but . . .'

'I'll break your neck if you've spoken to Serena about it!' he threatened, and meant it, ignoring the shocked stare of an old lady who had been about to sit down and quickly passed up the aisle.

'After your unseemly rush to get me out of the house, I couldn't possibly have had time to *say* anything to anybody, now could I?' Julia reasoned, but her smile was sly and secretive.

The guard's whistle blew before he could demand a further explanation, but he was inclined to believe that Julia's attempts at being enigmatic were not to be taken seriously; he wasted no time, however, in getting back to Rippondale.

His mother anxiously looked up as he strode purposefully into the lounge; she was finding the emotional turbulence of the last day a severe strain.

'Has she gone for good?'

'Yes,' he said shortly, not wishing to discuss the woman he had already dismissed from his mind. 'Where's Serena?'

'Hasn't come down yet. I suspect she needed a good night's sleep after the meal last night,' she said on a weary sigh. 'Come to that, you could be in need of the same.'

If she had expected any explanation for his haggard appearance, it was not forthcoming.

'I'm going to the study.'

Two hours and half a page later, Adam accepted the fact that he was unable to concentrate, for Serena intruded between each line. As he headed for the stables, his eyes were drawn upwards to her room. The curtains were drawn open and he wondered if she had already gone out somewhere and he had missed her.

So much for the hope that her long holidays might bring them closer, he thought bitterly as he saddled up the white stallion to go riding alone. This time he twisted the knife himself by speculating whether his supposed rejection would drive her into Saxon's arms, just as the last time when he had come so very near to losing his self-control.

He spurred the horse to the top of that hill where he had first kissed her—and recognised his sentimentality for what it was. As he gazed unseeingly at the valley below him, cool logic told him that a day might come when he would have outlived his usefulness to Serena. Perhaps he already had. He could just hear her saying, 'He's all yours'—tough and defiant. But on an emotional level he couldn't imagine how he would be able to cope with it.

He read no significance into her behaviour in the studio; in the cold light of day he couldn't believe she would have gone through with it. Another test, maybe? The exact motivation behind her offer eluded him—but it was not love. She had responded to him with passion, fierce and fiery, but never with that soft loving warmth that crept into her eyes and voice when she talked of her father.

It was after noon when he finally galloped home, with a recklessness that reflected his mood, and seeing the Mini parked at the front, he threw the reins to Brocklehurst, who had by now given up any pretension of being a gardener. With the curt, unnecessary instruction to rub White Lightning down, he found himself running up to the door of the house.

Without losing his sudden growing sense of panic at the sight of the Mini parked at such an odd angle, Adam dashed upstairs. The instant he reached Serena's bedroom, the truth began to steal over him like a cold paralysis. The twin photographs of her parents were gone and no brushes or perfume cluttered up the dressing-table. As if to deny what the bare surfaces and the stripped bedlinen were telling him, he opened the wardrobe, then turned from the empty hangers and caught his reflection in the inside mirror—his self-composure cracking wide to let all the naked agony come through.

That was Nancy's first thought when she muttered breathlessly, 'She's gone!'—only to see the look of defeat in his eyes. She had steeled herself for his anger, but not the utter dejection in his moan as he sank down on the bare mattress. 'It seems she left in the early hours of this morning, or so her college friend said when she brought the car back. She's written a note—it's addressed to me, but I think you should read it.' Nancy pressed the note into Adam's hand. 'I don't understand all of it—especially the reference to you.'

He had to read it twice before he could focus and make full sense of it.

'Dear Nancy,
    I hope you will forgive me for doing things this way, but I was frightened you'd try to dissuade me, and I've

kept you too long from your life back in London. Don't
worry—it's something I want to do. Fly solo. Go round
Europe and visit all the places I've dreamed about. Lots
of my college friends do it in the summer.

Tell Adam thanks—his debt is cancelled. I'll write
soon.

Serena.'

The letter fluttered from his hands as he anguishedly
gripped his head, his whole frame shaking with despair.
Nerves raw with a confusion of anger and desolation, he
couldn't stop his mind filling with changing visions of
her—Serena smiling, angry, fragile, mocking, beautiful—
the sound of her voice, compelling even when it uttered
words of cold dislike.

'Here, drink this.' Nancy Carmichael, having realised
her son was in shock, had gone for a large glass of brandy.
Placing the glass to his lips, she forced him to drink the
burning liquid. 'Adam,' she consoled, 'Adam, we need
you—Serena and I. Don't fall apart on us!'

The sound of Serena's name acted as more of a restora-
tive than the brandy, and his pride reasserted itself,
making him despise his show of weakness for a girl who
could breeze out of his life as abruptly as she had become a
part of it.

'That bitch doesn't need anyone. She's one hundred per
cent ice!'

'Don't, Adam,' Nancy pleaded, sitting down beside
him. 'You love her. Don't despise yourself for the emotion
or her for causing it.'

But she couldn't hold him as he rose and crossed to the
window, pretending an absorption with the view while he
tried to bring himself under some sort of control.

'You have to bring her back, Adam,' his mother
announced quietly, coming to his side.

It was a long time before he could form a reply, cold and
aloof.

'You read her note, Mother. She said my debt has been paid,' he clipped out, brushing past his mother on the way to the door.

Nancy trailed him to his room and watched a little startled as he opened and shut drawers, quickly and efficiently adding to the pile of clothes on his bed—far too many things for a short trip abroad!

'You're not going to fetch her back, are you?' she accused with a dawning horror.

No, he wasn't. He had the right to privacy too—a dark corner where he could nurse his wounds. He continued to pack methodically while he said grimly, 'No, Mother, don't ask that of me.'

'I'm frightened, Adam. She's so young . . .' Nancy appealed, and clung on to his arm until he turned and answered her.

'She'll survive. She's strong—she's had to be,' he said, and unconsciously his respect for Serena crept back into his voice. He remembered all the pointless cruelties she had been made to suffer. A shadow would come into her eyes and he'd say 'Tell me', and she would, sometimes sadly, with tears held back, at others angrily. Once she had said that no one would be allowed that close to hurt again. She had meant it. He should have listened.

'Because of Andrea?' Nancy pressed, and when his eyes hazed with memory, she decided to be open. 'Serena has never referred to her once in the last two years. At first I thought the loss was too new to be spoken of, but as time went on . . . well, it just wasn't natural. I hoped she'd tell me in time. I didn't want to force her after she drew back from Simon Clarke. But she chose you instead, didn't she?' She paused, but Adam didn't look as though he was going to give up any of Serena's secrets.

'I understand that. I've watched that special affinity you and Serena have for each other grow over the last months. No, Adam, don't stop me,' she raised a silencing hand when he would have denied it as an illusion which had deceived him too. 'Against all odds, it's there, and perhaps it's a good thing for both of you. But don't you see, it shuts the rest of us out. And I have the right to know—I love you both.'

He saw that their conspiracy of silence had hurt his mother by exclusion, but the motive for it was still there as he warned bleakly, 'It's not a pretty story.'

Her reaction was totally unexpected as she lost all patience with her clever confident son and came back staunchly, 'For God's sake, Adam Carmichael! I'm sixty-six years old, I've lived through a world war, and your father, as much as I loved him, wasn't always an easy man to be married to.'

The point was made, especially with her sudden reference to his father. He started economically and unemotionally, but by the end of the narrative his voice had broken with feeling.

'The marriage, as you suspected, had taken a bad turn very early on. Serena's last memory of her father was of him trying to reason Andrea out of another of her bitter tirades. Whether the argument contributed to the accident we'll never know, because Serena was stretched out on the back seat supposedly asleep, but when she came out of hospital, confused and grieving for her father, the last person she wanted to turn to for comfort was Andrea. She was no longer bound by her father's instructions to try and love Andrea, and perhaps it was this rejection that tipped the balance.

'At first the intimidation was silent—waking up in the middle of the night to find her stepmother watching her from the foot of the bed, saying nothing. A spook in the darkness that became part of a nightmare that came when Serena couldn't force herself to stay awake.

'And during the day, Andrea fussing, Andrea playing devoted stepmother by taking up all her meals and exacting a price for the bed and board she supplied. If Serena sat up and begged and licked the mistress's hand, then she'd get fed and patted for being a good girl. If not, she'd go hungry. Thank God, Andrea was still sane enough to keep her alive on scraps that didn't have to be begged for.

'With the passing of time Serena added her own refinements—she rolled over and played dead. Initially the switching off was a trick, but it was met with an increasingly violent response that made Serena want to stay as part of the dreams inside her head. Paradoxically the physical abuse kept her in touch with reality, but as it tailed off with Andrea's illness, the dreams almost took over completely—and then we came along . . .'

Nancy sat silent through it all, honour bound not to express her horror by her claim that she could take it, but when Adam finished so abruptly, she asked, aghast, 'How could anyone do that to a child?'

'Who knows?' Adam replied, but continued, 'A very sick sort of jealousy, I think. Serena came first with her father—the enchanting child given to him by the wife of his heart. Too late Andrea realised she came a poor third to the child and a ghost, unacceptable to the possessive woman she was. A devouring monster, that's what Serena called her—and with Templeton gone, she made damn sure she took it out on his child.'

His explanation was calm and rational, but underneath there was a bitter sympathy with Andrea's victim, and Nancy no longer doubted the quality and strength of Adam's love.

'Why didn't she tell anybody?' she murmured bewilderedly.

'She did,' he returned with aggression, and cancelled it with a rueful smile when he realised he was being oversensitive to criticism of Serena, his earlier anger against her dissipated. 'She told a governess, who promptly went to Andrea to report the lies of her ungrateful charge. An old buffer of a doctor, who listened and promised to help her. He did—with a bottle of sedatives to calm the poor child. And Andrea took her retribution—with drugs and humiliations she made sure Serena didn't risk telling any more tales. She belonged to Andrea. No one else cared. Even in death Andrea was pounding over her total dependence with a legacy to her *beloved* stepdaughter of Serena's own mother's jewellery. And I, for my sins, was nominated new keeper.'

For a long moment his mother sat in stunned silence as the full picture came home to her, then she rose, very pale, very shaken, to excuse herself.

Left alone, Adam didn't finish his packing but went downstairs to the lounge. He poured himself a whisky with the cynical thought that he was starting as he meant to go on. But he took a long time to drink it. Calmer now, more able to think, he no longer found that farewell note convincing and feared for the unpredictable wild side of Serena's nature. Or maybe he just preferred to believe she couldn't walk away from him, cool and uncaring, without saying goodbye.

'Adam! Adam!' His mother's voice, loud and insistent, broke into his absorption.

'Feeling better?' he asked, knowing how sick he had felt when he had heard only a fragment of the truth.

'Yes.' She dismissed tersely. 'Listen to me, Adam. Tomorrow. You'll go tomorrow and bring her back.'

It was a command, and he wasn't arguing but simply stating facts when he said, 'I don't see how you think I could force her to come back with me.'

'Then at least go and find out why she left. She'll tell you, Adam. She's shared so much with you already.'

'Father confessor,' he laughed self-mockingly. 'I can't go on playing that role any more.'

'I'm not asking you to.' Nancy had done her own thinking upstairs, and awarded him a hard, searching glance before challenging him outright, 'Did you ever tell her you loved her?'

'It was bloody obvious if she'd cared to see it,' he growled, his bitterness defending his reticence.

She shook her head, a gesture of maternal despair. 'For a highly intelligent man you can be incredibly stupid!'

It was an echo that brought an image of a vulnerable hurting Serena from the previous night; God, how he ached to hold her!

'She doesn't say where she's gone.' As a protest it was weak and his mother bowled it over with a dogged vehemence.

'I checked with the airports. She took the noon flight to Rome from Manchester. She's heading for a small Italian fishing village in the South. And it's no pleasure trip she's on.'

A pilgrimage home, his mother meant, that could turn out to be one more disappointment. 'You trust me with her?' Adam asked, recalling her hostility in the past.

'I trust you to ignore your own inclinations, and do what Serena wishes—whatever it is,' she responded cryptically, and waited tensely for his decision.

'I'll go,' he conceded quietly, incapable of promising more.

And scarcely heard his mother murmuring, 'You'll do the right thing, Adam. I know you will.'

CHAPTER ELEVEN

YESTERDAY had been spent travelling and snatching fitful sleep when she could, and today facing up to the realisation that there was no such thing for her as home. The village hadn't changed, but home was not a place, but people. And they were gone—everybody she had ever needed to stay close. Even Adam, although she hadn't been able to take waiting around for the final parting. Lucky Adam who didn't depend on anybody.

Serena had tried to hold on to him a little while longer, and had made a complete fool of herself by imagining he would still want her that way. One kiss, his hand gentle on her breast, and all that frightening panic raised by his goodbye present had dissolved, lost in mindless beautiful sensation till there was just Adam and that moment and his loving.

But he had merely been teaching her another object lesson, drawing away from her, cold and insulting, untouched by it all. When her body had been crying out to him to make her his woman, he had rejected her with his scathing, 'I don't make love to children.'

She had lain on her bed, dry-eyed and nursing the hurt he had inflicted, and much later when she had heard his door shutting at the other side of the stairs, she had conceived the absurd idea of going to him to apologise for embarrassing him with her floundering efforts to be adult about her feelings for him.

The apology had never been made. Frozen in the passageway outside her door, she had watched that awful woman walking down from Adam's room, her face flushed and her sullen mouth forming a smile when she spotted Serena. The smile had said it all, and yet she hadn't

believed it. Not at first. She had sat on her windowseat
numb to the pain, but it hadn't worked for long because
she had never been able to shut out Adam.

Her pride had changed the hurting to anger and sent
her running. Anger with him, with the unfairness of it. She
could have loved him better than that cold selfish woman
if he'd just shown her the way. Didn't he know that?
Couldn't he see? And she wouldn't have put a price on her
love but left him free to come and go.

Serena drifted in from the balcony. At last the sun was
setting and she left the shutters open for the breeze, but
hesitated about putting on the light.

The hotel looked a little less shabby in the half-light—it
was the only hotel in the village, cheap and clean, and the
proprietor's wife, remembering the Signora Templeton
who had once been part of the small community, had
made Serena feel very welcome.

But with the night her loneliness began—she had to
stay angry, to cut *him* out of her life. She had to do it to
survive. Tomorrow she'd move on, use the money her
mother's aunt had left her to see Europe, as she'd said in
the note.

The knock at her door interrupted the forced exercise of
planning a grand tour for which she had no enthusiasm,
and she pulled her towelling robe tighter as she went to
answer the call of 'Signorina Templeton?'

Her automatic smile froze on her lips as she took in
Adam standing at the proprietor's side. For a second, she
considered slamming the door, leaving him to try and
explain her conduct.

'*Signorina,* your cousin, he arrive with the sad news
of the family,' the unwitting hotelkeeper repeated the
lie designed to dispel his suspicion of Adam's sudden
arrival.

Serena's startled eyes locked on Adam's and anger
quickly replaced relief at the slight shake of his head and
his taking up the pretence with, 'Aunt Ida, I'm afraid,

passed away in her sleep.' He willed her to follow his lead, to reassure the manager of his right to be there.

And she did. Eventually. Coming back with a sharp, 'Well, which of us gets the old dear's money?'

The Italian, with his innate reverence of the family and of the dead, was truly shocked by her hard words; she had seemed such a nice young lady.

Adam, on the other hand, knew she was trying to embarrass him, but he snatched the opportunity it presented.

'As you can hear, *signore*, my dear cousin has no need for your protection,' he effectively dismissed the other man, who was more than willing to let the heartless English get on with their own affairs.

His foot was in the door, too quick for her hurried attempt to close it on him. She gave up the struggle and retreated to the bed.

'You've outraged the poor man's sensibilities with that peculiar sense of humour,' Adam muttered, not really giving a damn about it.

'Why are you here?' she asked icily. 'I didn't leave so you would follow.'

Why indeed, when she was staring at him as though she wished him in hell. 'My mother was worried about you.' It sounded lame even to his ears, but he was feeling his way, scared of treading on sacred ground.

'As you can see, I'm quite capable of finding a bed for the night. Your duty's accomplished, you can go home,' she said tautly.

Aware as he was of her nakedness beneath the towelling robe, Adam could still see the wounded child that lurked under the seemingly hard exterior. About to move away from the door, he checked himself; this was as near as he trusted himself.

'My mother wants you to come home.'

'I have my own life to live, and that pile of rubble was never *my* home,' she declared, a shade more defensively.

In all probability what she said was true, and he had no clever arguments to counter that sad fact. He said what was in his heart.

'*I* want you home, Princess.'

It brought her eyes back to his face, wide in their anger, as she flung contemptuously at him, 'I would have thought one woman was enough for you. In the same house anyway.'

'Julia left yesterday morning,' he announced quietly. 'She has no place in my life, now or in the future.'

'Not even as a casual companion for the night?'

Her bitterness was unmistakable, yet he dismissed the fleeting hope to which it gave rise, frightened he was reading into it only what he wanted to be there.

'I haven't been to bed with Julia or any other woman for over a year,' he stated plainly.

'I *saw* her,' Serena accused, her voice rising. 'I saw her at your door!'

'You saw her entering or leaving?'

'Leaving your room,' she threw at him, her rigid composure cracking. She shut her eyes tightly against him, crying, 'For pity's sake, Adam, don't deny it. Spare me that!'

But he couldn't. It was too important, and this time he had to risk her bad opinion.

'If you saw her leaving, then it must have been shortly after twelve. And whatever you may think, it's not my habit to make love to a woman and then turf her out of my bed in the middle of the night. I want her beside me in the morning,' he finished softly, his mind filled with the clear beautiful vision of Serena lying with him.

'Stop!' she cried tempestuously. 'I don't want to hear any more!'

'No, you'll listen to what I have to say. I did not ask her to come to my room. She got the idea I'd welcome her from some cheeky little madame in a temper,' Adam accused, and startled a blush from her before she flung herself face down on the pillow and tried to block out the sound of his voice. Without thinking, he crossed to the bed and dragged her round.

'Nor did I make love to her. Trust me, Princess. I wouldn't lie to you.' He had thought her still angry, but when he saw her long lashes, darker than her hair and wet with the tears that threatened, he touched her cheek tenderly with the back of his hand. 'Don't cry, Princess. I can't bear it. I'll go now and we'll talk again in the morning.'

When he would have risen to leave her, a small desperate hand clutched his arm.

'Stay with me. Hold me.' Her plea was but a whisper, yet Serena had no doubts about what she wanted. A memory she could live on, to join her collection of transient dreams.

'You don't know what you're asking,' Adam didn't feel noble, but his conscience stirred deep within him. 'I can't . . .' he forced the words out, his breathing ragged with his desire for her.

'You don't want me?' she asked with the directness of her generation.

'Very much. I want you very . . .' He was silenced by the arms that slid around his neck, and the mouth that pressed tentatively on his, with a kiss that spoke of nervous shyness. The hands that gripped her waist with the intention of pushing her gently away were alive to her perfumed softness and they betrayed him, drawing her closer until only their clothing separated them. Still he felt the strength within him to resist temptation.

And then all was sensation, momentarily obscuring right and wrong, as Serena's fingers curled into his hair, and her mouth moved beneath his, desperately searching for a response. Her lips opened fully as he pushed her slowly down on the bed, and the taste of her was awakening a hunger that made his body tremble. But he was afraid—afraid of damaging his frail, beautiful Princess.

He eased her away from him and they lay on their sides on the large double bed, not touching with their bodies, but communicating with their eyes. She looked so open, so sure—there was no fear in her steady smile.

'What about tomorrow?' he murmured hesitantly.

She brushed her fingers against his lips. 'Shh! No tomorrows. There's just now. Just us.'

Reverently he undressed her, and then himself, and for a long moment they were silent, motionless shadows in the darkening room, each anticipating but shying from disappointing the other. Stretching his hand out, he slowly traced the outline of her face, his fingers trailed the length of her body. He wanted the touch of all of her, to know her by heart. Lifting her hand, he brought it to his mouth and kissed the babysoft palm, causing a low moan to escape her lips. He was on fire for her, yet restrained the urge to cover her body with his and use her to end his suffering; more than anything he wished to pleasure her, show her how much he loved her.

With a featherlight touch he explored the smoothness of her thighs, wondering at the flawlessness of her small body. And then with hesitating shyness, Serena guided his hand upwards until it covered her firm rounded breast, and its hardness told him of her excitement. Lowering his head, he took its peak in his mouth, slowly teasing it to full life, glorying in the pleasure noises it brought to her lips until he could stand no more. Frantically his mouth sought hers and forced it open, no longer able to check his ardency as he plundered and drained its sweetness.

Nothing had prepared him for the ecstasy of complete possession when their bodies fused into one, but it was ephemeral, replaced by a dreadful shaming agony at her muffled cry of pain, confirming that her denial of innocence had been an illusion. When he would have left her, her hands urged him to love her, to take all he wanted from her, and his flesh ignored the dictates of his mind, bringing him to a fulfilment that was shattering in its impact.

Afterwards they lay in silence, save for the sound of their strained breathing, fingers entwined like diffident children.

Adam turned to face her, eyes adjusting to the darkness, and looked on her with adoration. For a second a shadow seemed to cross her eyes, but she made the moment perfect with a quiet contented smile that said no regrets, no recriminations.

Softly he whispered, 'Forgive me. I hurt you.'

Serena moved into his arms and laid her tousled head on his hair-coarsened chest. 'No, it was . . . it was beautiful.'

Stroking her hair, he was filled with a wondering gratitude for the gift she had bestowed on him. He couldn't let himself believe that there would not be a lifetime of tomorrows with his lovely, loving girl.

Her even breathing told him she was asleep and, at peace with himself for the first time in so long, Adam slept too.

She flitted through his dreams—an elusive spectral creature, beckoning with her beauty but impossible to capture. As he drifted into semi-consciousness he reached out for her in the coming dawn—his living, breathing Serena, seeking the reassurance that she had not disappeared with the night. His hand travelled over the cold empty space where she had lain and a panicked voice, unrecognisable as his own, cried out her name.

Within minutes he was dressed and in the hotel lobby, pressing notes on a bemused night porter who informed him that the young lady had already left for the station.

The platform was deserted, save for a lone porter whose faltering English painfully established that there was no train until nine. And yes, a young lady had left a case with him before she left the station for the path that led to the village cemetery.

As Adam climbed the hillside, he passed an ancient disused church, and once inside the cemetery, his eyes were drawn to the grave whose headstone of white marble dominated the west wall. Of Serena there was no sign.

Something compelled him towards the headstone, and his eyes riveted on the small miniature set in the large cross that rose from its base. Serena's face stared back at him—the same breathtaking beauty he had let slip from his arms while he slept.

Bending down, he read the inscription:

MORAG CAMPBELL TEMPLETON
1943–1970
BELOVED WIFE OF GRAHAM
AND LOVING MOTHER OF SERENA JANE

'AND I WILL LOVE YOU STILL, MY DEAR,
TILL A' THE SEAS GANG DRY'

And now he understood perfectly how Graham Templeton could do nothing other than keep that promise to a beautiful young wife, even if he had so tragically tried to fill the emptiness her leaving had created.

He heard her before she rounded the corner of the church with her arms full of flowers. Her hair was tied back from her face—a fresh and lovely vision in her simple white cotton dress.

For a moment she was unaware of his presence and he caught a glimpse of the woman she would be in maturity, fulfilling all the promise of her name. And then it was gone, chased away by her first sight of him and the dark troubled expression displacing the contentment. She hovered, ready for flight, as he slowly uncoiled to his full height and backed away from the grave. This she did not wish to share with him.

And while he stood a hundred yards away, watching her as she knelt by the stone to arrange her flowers, a fear grew in him that she had not intended sharing anything with him ever again. He recalled her assertion of the night before—'I did not leave so you would follow'. Somehow he had lost her, and he could not fathom why.

Serena sat motionless, staring at the portrait, reliving memories, fleeting but precious, of her childhood. When she finally moved away, there was a suspicion of tears on her cheeks. Adam walked a few paces behind her through the rusty cemetery gate and down the hill, sensing that she did not wish him to speak. Just before the village she abruptly halted and without turning, said clearly, tonelessly,

'Please, Adam, go away.'

He stood immobile, unable to move, to find the will to act. She wheeled round on him, a small figure of defiance dwarfed by his height.

'What do you want of me? What more? I played the game by your rules, right up until the end. But you keep changing them, and I just can't keep up.' Her voice was heavy with pain and bewilderment.

'Rules?' he repeated stupidly.

'Yes, your damned rules! I've tried to be your sort of woman. I've made no ugly scenes . . . didn't ask for more than one night.' Her eyes pleaded with him. 'Please—just go away before you spoil it.'

Didn't she know how he felt? Hadn't he shown her more clearly than words could ever hope to that he didn't want just a memory?

'I want to marry you,' he blurted out in desperation, the words halting her in amazement as she gasped, 'Because I was a virgin?'

'If you had a score of lovers before me, it wouldn't have changed anything. I'd still want to marry you,' he muttered intensely. '—And it's not very flattering my proposal is greeted with tears. A simple yes or no would do.'

With the back of her hand Serena scrubbed away the errant tears, and refused to meet his eyes as she whispered, 'I can't marry you, Adam, I can't . . .'

Stung and confused, he growled, 'I won't be used as a sex object for you to cut your teeth on, Serena!' Even to his own ears it came out cruel and ridiculous.

She laughed without humour. 'That's my line, surely. Except that your teeth are sharp enough already.'

They had reverted to being antagonists, and yet strangely he felt stronger with the shift in mood.

'I don't know what you mean,' he said, temper rising. 'Why can't you be bloody honest for a change?'

'I don't know what *you* mean,' she replied crossly.

'Don't throw smokescreens of other women and make me out the villain so you can carry on playing Snow White.' He grasped one arm, his fingers savagely biting into her bare flesh. 'Admit it. You wanted sex and I was merely a bystander.'

The hard slap she delivered on his cheek, an instinctive reaction to his cruel words, cracked wide his control; his hand gripped her long hair, forcing her head up. Ready to receive his brutal retaliation, her green eyes seemed enormous in their fear, defusing his anger until only his love for her remained. His kiss was one of ineffable tenderness, devoid of passion, a promise to cherish. He cupped her face in his hands and imagined he saw his love reflected in her eyes, no longer fearful, but wondering; and then, as though she could no longer bear the intensity of his gaze, Serena buried her head in his shoulder, her arms curling round his waist. He cradled her small frame in his arms, unable to tell which one of them was trembling more.

'Will you marry me?' His voice quavered. She did not respond, but he felt the slight shake of the head against his chest. 'Why not?'

Her words were muffled but distinguishable. 'Because I love you.'

What a time for her to pick to make one of her obscure remarks! Adam groaned inwardly.

Pushing her at arm's length, he demanded with more than a tinge of offended pride, 'Are you saying that because you imagine that's what I want to hear? I want to marry you. For us to be together for the rest of our lives, and you give me a loving lie as a consolation prize!'

She pulled away from him completely and shot him a look of pure exasperation before stating, 'I said you could be incredibly stupid sometimes!'

'How am I supposed to know you love me?' he challenged brusquely. 'You've talked about your father as though he was one step short of a god, and you stand there scowling at me as if I was the devil himself.'

'Ooh!' The sigh was drawn out, and then she was stalking away from him, but this time Adam had no doubts about following, and when he spun her round, she flared up at him, 'You're not my father, Adam Carmichael, and I don't want you to be! And maybe in your sophisticated circles, making love is just one move away from a handshake. But to me it's an expression of love, and I showed you last night in your bed how I love you!'

She was positively glaring at him, her confession of love delivered with a strange fury, but he believed and was overwhelmed by it—the realisation that she had been willing to settle for so much less than she should ever deserve in order to give him the freedom she imagined he wanted.

Curling his fingers round one wrist, Adam dragged her to the shaded privacy of the woodland bordering the road and stifled her protest with the kiss of a lover, moulding her body tightly into his so she could feel his need for her.

When he finally released her, she was breathless and blushing furiously, and he stared fixedly at her enchanting face, wondering if it would always hurt just to look at her.

'Adam!' she tried to break into his daze, snapping to gain his attention. 'Stop looking at me that way. It's indecent!'

'You'll have to get used to it, Princess,' he laughed down at her cross expression, feeling heady with the scent of victory, 'because I won't be looking at anyone else but you for the next fifty years. Afterwards, who knows?'

'We have to be sensible,' she protested with a heavy frown for his teasing. 'We have nothing in common.'

'A fierce pride, a slightly warped sense of humour tinged with sarcasm, a determination to get our own way,' he listed with questionable seriousness, and as a pretended afterthought, 'Oh, and love. And let's face it, with a combination like that, who else would be happy with either of us?'

Serena ducked away from the mouth making a disruptive trail down her neck, struggling to be clear-sighted in the face of his frivolity. 'Our life styles? I hate parties.'

'So do I. Lots of boring people talking for the sake of it. We'll go and live on a desert island, just the two of us.'

'Children?' she challenged his remark about there being just the two of them.

'Six at least,' he quipped, and then on a lower, more serious note, 'Well, however many it takes to produce a little girl that looks exactly like her beautiful mother.'

She was losing the battle, but somehow she didn't mind any more, her protests growing weaker by the second.

'We don't share the same interests.'

'You like classical music, don't you?' Serena nodded her assent. 'Well, so do I. Especially Beethoven.' He'd seen her record collection. 'Who's your favourite author, besides myself of course?'

At last she was smiling, as she played his game, 'J.D. Salinger.'

'Mine too,' Adam avowed, making a mental note to remedy the fact that he had never read any of the writer in question.

But she was wise to him. 'Which painter do you admire the most?'

He frowned with concentration, as though debating the merits of the great masters, and then, with slow deliberation, announced, 'Serena Templeton *Carmichael*.'

She smiled up at him, and he sensed in that moment that she had put her trust on him. The game was over; they were both winners—after all, it turned out they were both on the same side. And shyly Serena laid her head once more on his chest, as though that was where she felt safest.

Quietly she whispered, not a question but a reassurance to both of them, 'For ever.'

' "Till all the seas gang dry," ' he quoted softly as his mouth brushed her forehead.